THE SHOOTING SCRIPT

SIDEWAYS

SCREENPLAY BY **ALEXANDER PAYNE** & **JIM TAYLOR**
BASED ON THE NOVEL BY **REX PICKETT**

INTRODUCTION BY **PETER TRAVERS**
AFTERWORD BY **REX PICKETT**

A Newmarket Shooting Script® Series Book
NEWMARKET PRESS • NEW YORK

The Newmarket Shooting Script® Series is a registered trademark of
Newmarket Publishing & Communications Company.

This book is published simultaneously in the United States of America and in Canada.

FIRST EDITION

10 9 8 7 6 5 4 3 2 1

ISBN: 1-55704-655-7

Library of Congress Catalog-in-Publication Data is available upon request.

QUANTITY PURCHASES

Companies, professional groups, clubs, and other organizations may qualify for special terms when ordering quantities
of this title. For information, write to Special Sales, Newmarket Press, 18 East 48th Street, New York, NY 10017;
call (212) 832-3575 or 1-800-669-3903; FAX (212) 832-3629; or e-mail mailbox@newmarketpress.com.

Website: www.newmarketpress.com

Manufactured in the United States of America.

OTHER BOOKS IN THE NEWMARKET SHOOTING SCRIPT® SERIES INCLUDE:

About a Boy: The Shooting Script
Adaptation: The Shooting Script
The Age of Innocence: The Shooting Script
American Beauty: The Shooting Script
Ararat: The Shooting Script
A Beautiful Mind: The Shooting Script
Big Fish: The Shooting Script
The Birdcage: The Shooting Script
Blackhawk Down: The Shooting Script
Cast Away: The Shooting Script
Dead Man Walking: The Shooting Script
Dreamcatcher: The Shooting Script
Erin Brockovich: The Shooting Script
Eternal Sunshine of the Spotless Mind:
    The Shooting Script
Gods and Monsters: The Shooting Script
Gosford Park: The Shooting Script
Human Nature: The Shooting Script

The Ice Storm: The Shooting Script
Igby Goes Down: The Shooting Script
I ♥ Huckabees: The Shooting Script
Knight's Tale: The Shooting Script
Man on the Moon: The Shooting Script
The Matrix: The Shooting Script
Nurse Betty: The Shooting Script
Pieces of April: The Shooting Script
The People vs. Larry Flynt: The Shooting Script
Punch-Drunk Love: The Shooting Script
Red Dragon: The Shooting Script
The Shawshank Redemption: The Shooting Script
Snatch: The Shooting Script
Snow Falling on Cedars: The Shooting Script
State and Main: The Shooting Script
Sylvia: The Shooting Script
Traffic: The Shooting Script
The Truman Show: The Shooting Script

OTHER NEWMARKET PICTORIAL MOVIEBOOKS AND NEWMARKET INSIDER FILM BOOKS INCLUDE:

The Age of Innocence: A Portrait of the Film★
Ali: The Movie and The Man★
Amistad: A Celebration of the Film by Steven Spielberg
The Art of The Matrix★
The Art of X2★
Bram Stoker's Dracula: The Film and the Legend★
Catch Me If You Can: The Illustrated Screenplay★
Chicago: The Movie and Lyrics★
Cold Mountain: The Journey from Book to Film
Crouching Tiger, Hidden Dragon: A Portrait of the Ang Lee Film★
Dances with Wolves: The Illustrated Story of the Epic Film★
E.T. The Extra Terrestrial From Concept to Classic—The Illustrated
    Story of the Film and the Filmmakers★
Frida: Bringing Frida Kahlo's Life and Art to Film★

Gladiator: The Making of the Ridley Scott Epic Film
Gods and Generals: The Illustrated Story of the Epic Civil War Film★
The Hulk: The Illustrated Screenplay★
In America: A Portrait of the Film★
The Jaws Log
Kinsey: Public and Private ★
Planet of the Apes: Re-imagined by Tim Burton★
Ray: A Tribute to the Movie, the Music and the Man★
Saving Private Ryan: The Men, The Mission, The Movie
The Sense and Sensibility Screenplay & Diaries★
Stuart Little: The Art, the Artists and the Story Behind the Amazing
    Movie★
Van Helsing: The Making of the Legend★
Vanity Fair: Bringing Thackeray's Timeless Novel to the Screen★

★Includes Screenplay

CONTENTS

INTRODUCTION

BY PETER TRAVERS

Since I am a film critic who firmly believes that director Alexander Payne and his writing partner Jim Taylor have turned Rex Pickett's novel *Sideways* into a transcendent human comedy and one of the best movies of the year, you might well ask: If the movie is such hot stuff, why do I need to read the screenplay?

Simple answer: Because they pair up beautifully.

In Hollywood, where formula is king, a screenplay exists mostly as a blueprint for cinematic explosions and headbanging. But if you do it right—Payne and Taylor do it very right, indeed, through their artful blend of characterization, dialogue and telling detail—the screenplay and the film can harmonize to create something fresh and intoxicating: different flavors emerge, dynamics change, understanding deepens, pleasures intensify. It doesn't happen often, of course. But it does happen with *Sideways*. Read the screenplay you have in your hands before or after you see the movie, and it's like pairing oysters with an ethereal Chablis, a rare steak with a powerful, exalting Cabernet.

The wine metaphor is apt. *Sideways* is drunk on wine, on its allure, its fragility, its vocabulary. Miles Raymond, the self-loathing, self-medicating sadsack brought to brilliant screen life by Paul Giamatti, has been officially depressed for two years—that's when his wife left him. He is stagnant in his job teaching English to eighth-graders, anxious that his novel will never collect anything but rejection slips, and bitter that his wife has remarried and seems—yikes!—happy. But not even Xanax and Lexapro can dull the passion Miles feels for the grape. Just the aroma of a fine wine snaps him back to life. He puts his nose right in the glass and inhales like a junkie. It's wine that motivates Miles to go away with his lifelong friend Jack Lopate, played by Thomas Haden Church, for a week of male bonding before Jack's wedding at which Miles will serve as best man. The plan is for Miles and Jack, a former soap actor now doing commercials, to drive away from Los Angeles and head for the Santa Ynez wine country, north of Santa Barbara, for a tasting tour. Never mind that Jack chews gum while tasting wines that he barely distinguishes as red or white. He just wants to get laid.

Talk about formula. On the surface, *Sideways* has all the makings of a bottom-feeding buddy farce—a forty-something *American Pie* in which the guys drink themselves sideways, play golf and pick up hotties who pour wine in the tasting centers along the stunning Santa Ynez Valley, which opens toward the Pacific. Hollywood would love to make that movie. Alexander Payne, bless him, would rather die.

You have to understand a few things about Payne before you can understand why *Sideways* works like a charm on screen. Back in 1986, Payne, now forty-three, once appeared in a short film called *How to Judge Character by the Face*. Meeting Payne for the first time recently in Manhattan at a Greek restaurant—it's only appropriate since his family name is Papadopoulos—I'm struck first by his eyes, alive with intelligent curiosity and mischief. Those qualities also characterize his movies, which until *Sideways* all took place around Omaha, Nebraska, where he was born and raised. At lunch, Payne orders the food (fish) and the wine (I won't tell you the varietal for fear of giving too much away about his personality) and talks vino and movies with equal brio.

Payne may have hit puberty in the *Star War/Jaws* era, but the filmmakers that excite him are such old masters as Akira Kurosawa, Luis Buñuel, and that incomparable Viennese cynic Billy Wilder, especially the comic-ash residue of Wilder's little-known *Ace in the Hole*. Payne came to film study at UCLA only after majoring in Spanish and history at Stanford. His student films quickly caught the attention of studio fatcats, which led to his 1996 debut film *Citizen Ruth*, starring Laura Dern as a pregnant paint sniffer who hilariously exploits both sides of the abortion issue. The controversial film never found a wide audience, despite the marketing force at Miramax and critical acclaim for Payne. Most young directors hit the sophomore jinx when they next step up at bat. But *Election*, in 1999, only made good on the promise Payne showed in *Citizen Ruth*. Reese Witherspoon gave the performance of her career to date as a high-school overachiever running for class president with the tenacity of Karl Rove. Paramount tried to sell this sharp political satire as a teen flick and failed. Payne had better luck in 2002 with *About Schmidt*, thanks to Jack Nicholson's Oscar-nominated performance as a retired Nebraska actuary with no life to look back on. Payne and Taylor were both nominated as well for their screenplay from a Louis Begley novel about a Manhattan attorney who bears scant resemblance to the Schmidt on screen. Payne doesn't deny he has battle scars from fighting with studios to keep his vision intact. He admits to having a secret weapon. "The right of final cut," he says. "I don't leave home without it."

It's typical of Payne that the follow-up to his biggest commercial success would be a film as modest-seeming as *Sideways*. There are no bankable movie stars, just superb actors. No high concept to sell it, just superior execution. No audience pandering, just trust in audience intelligence. When you buy a bottle of wine you look at the label. It tells you where the grapes were grown and by whom. It's a way to help identify quality wines. A movie with the Alexander Payne label carries that same sign of quality.

Is too much being made of the fact that *Sideways* is the first Payne movie to be filmed outside of his native Nebraska? Could be. Payne says he shot his first three movies close to home because "I hadn't seen the Midwest in a movie before." And because he knew that area, he could take a tip from his beloved Italian neo-realists (Fellini, DeSica, Bertolucci) and keep it real. God knows the Santa Ynez wine country has hardly been overworked by Hollywood. Payne and Taylor visited the area with novelist Rex Pickett and, as ever, Payne keeps it real. His director of photography Phedon Papamichael catches the natural beauty of the vineyards, but avoids the postcard-pretty *Under the Tuscan Sun* depiction that's supposed to prompt audiences to call their travel agents. No attempt is made to make the area or its people larger than life. Normal life, with all its routine pain, offbeat humor, and freakish variety, suits Payne just fine, thank you. Payne has described *Sideways* as "a little comedy about deluded people." Last time I looked, that encompassed most of us.

Here's where it should be pointed out that Miles and Jack have company on their odyssey—two women who stir up the plot. Watch someone who knows his wine, and you'll see him set a glass down and swirl it vigorously in tight circles, almost to the point of spillage. That volatizes the esters. As Miles explains to Jack, this oxygenating process "gets some air into the wine, opens it up and unlocks the aroma and the flavors." That's what the addition of Stephanie and Maya do to *Sideways*. Maya, played by Virginia Madsen (the bombshell from such 1980s movies as *The Hot Spot,* here in a smashing comeback), is a waitress at a local restaurant; she's gorgeous, newly divorced, wine-obsessed, and interested in Miles if he had the guts to get past small talk. It's Jack who intercedes. He sets up a double-date by flirting with Maya's sassy friend Stephanie, a single mom who pours wine for the tourist tasters. As played by Sandra Oh, an exemplary actress born in Canada to Korean parents and Payne's wife since 2003, Stephanie is Jack's equal at carnal come-ons. Jack neglects to tell Stephanie about his wedding plans, and Miles reluctantly goes along with the deception, setting up a moral conflict that plays against the laughs, notably the comic tour de force of a dinner scene with the two couples, in which a tipsy, slurring Miles excuses himself to phone his ex-wife with teary recriminations. Jack calls this no-no "D&D," meaning drink and dial, and gives Miles hell for it. The scene reads funny and plays funnier thanks to Payne's mastery at lacing the humor with tinges of heartbreak. Payne is not a sentimentalist—tearjerking is thankfully not in his arsenal—but his astringent style that makes the fainter of heart pucker at its harshness never shuts off genuine emotion. He feels for these four characters, and we do as well.

The byline on the *Sideways* shooting script includes only the names of Payne and Taylor, but both writers know deep down they have four uncredited collaborators named Giamatti, Church, Oh, and Madsen. To see *Sideways* on screen and then re-read the script—a worthwhile pursuit, by the way, tantamount to quaffing a great wine and then pouring another glass to savor it—is to have those actors locked in your mind. Take the character of Jack, for starters. As written in the novel and the script, Jack is pretty much a pig. He cheats on his bride to be, not just with Stephanie, but with a chubby waitress he seduces, well, just because he can. His fame as Dr. Derek Summersby on that TV soap gets him access to women he is happy to exploit. He acts the role of lover to Stephanie, charming her young daughter and her mother and telling them what a great life they could all have together out here in god's wine country. When Stephanie, learning of his lies, beats him breathless with her motorcycle helmet, you want to cheer. Jack is impossible to like.

Except on screen, where Thomas Haden Church—best known for TV roles on such shows as *Wings* and *Ned and Stacey*—makes Jack impossible *not* to like. Church does more than catch Jack's fun-loving enthusiasm, he finds the delusion that drives it. "He's an actor," Miles tells Maya to explain Jack's duplicity, "he believes what he says when he says it." Jack doesn't want to face the hard truth that his upcoming marriage to an Armenian princess will mark the end of his failing career. He knows he'll end up working for his wife's rich father, a life that will dry out the studly scenarios he uses to hide behind. There's a sadness in Jack, a desperation, and Church nails it. Just as Oh makes Stephanie a fully dimensional character instead of a clichéd babe easy to dismiss as another of Jack's conquests. The actors give us people capable of receiving and inflicting emotional bruises, and no one is off the hook.

Least of all Miles. Giamatti, so extraordinary in *American Splendor* and customarily the best thing about every movie he's in, hits a career peak in the role. Payne and Taylor give him a transfixing moment—not in the novel—of self-revelation. Typically, Miles doesn't know it, he thinks he's describing why he loves Pinot Noir more than any wine on the planet. "It's a hard grape to grow," he tells Maya. "It's thin-skinned, temperamental. It's not a survivor like Cabernet that can grow and thrive anywhere. . . and withstand neglect. Pinot's only happy in specific little corners of the world, and it needs a lot of doting. Only the most patient and faithful and caring growers can do it, can access Pinot's achingly beautiful qualities. It doesn't come to you. You have to come to it, see?"

Maya sees all right, but she's impatient with Miles. She can't believe he's been hording a 1961 Cheval Blanc (one of the greatest Bordeaux), waiting for the special occasion to drink it. Maya hits him hard on that one. "You know what I think?" she asks. "I think the day you open a '61 Cheval Blanc, that's the special occasion." It's impossible, I think, to overpraise Virginia Madsen's radiant performance as Maya. It's not just a part that should put her in the lead position in the Oscar race for a Best Supporting Actress, it's a breakthrough part that should give her a whole new career. The years have made her beauty richer, her grasp of character more subtle and affect-ing. And she has the film's most moving speech—again, not in the novel—that defines herself through wine.

"I started to appreciate the life of wine," she tells Miles, "that it's a living thing, that it connects you more to life. I like to think about what was going on the year the grapes were growing. I like to think about how the sun was shining that summer and what the weather was like. I think about all those people who tended and picked the grapes. And if it's an old wine, how many of them must be dead by now. I love how wine continues to evolve, how every time I open a bottle the wine will taste different than if I uncorked it on any other day, or at any other moment. A bottle of wine is like life itself—it grows up, evolves and gains complexity. Then it peaks—like your '61—and begins its steady, inexorable decline. And it tastes so fucking good."

You read those words or hear the actors say them on screen, and you real-ize that Payne and Taylor have given us classic movie love story about two people who can only express their feelings through the language of wine.

In one scene, while Stephanie and Jack rip each other's clothes off in another room, Miles and Maya examine Stephanie's wine collection in an erotic dance that's better than sex.

Maya peers at a 2000 La Rinconada: "That's tempting," says Miles. "But shouldn't we hold back on that for a few years? It's pretty massive." Maya then slides out a 1990 Eschevaux, then slides it back in. "Nah," she tells Miles. "I don't think we know each other well enough."

And so it goes. *Sideways* may create a run on wine stores with couples eager to try out the wines that bring Miles and Maya together. Go ahead, mark the pages of the script, and go shopping. But even if you know less about wine than Jack, who can't tell a Pinot Noir from a film noir, *Sideways* has a way of sneaking up and knocking you flat the more you see yourself in the characters.

Payne isn't immune. Maya's crack about her ex-husband ("he had a big, kind of show-off cellar") could be Payne mulling the mindless Hollywood blockbusters that crowd the multiplex. His palate is sharper than that, and he wants ours to be as well. He's like Miles decrying Merlot ("If anyone orders Merlot, I'm leaving") as a mass-produced grape lacking in balance, depth and complexity. All those rare things that make themselves felt in *Sideways*.

So break out the '61 Cheval Blanc for Alexander Payne. He makes watching movies—and reading them—a special occasion.

Sideways

by Alexander Payne & Jim Taylor
based on the novel by Rex Pickett

May 29, 2003

UNDER THE STUDIO LOGO:

KNOCKING at a door and distant dog BARKING.

NOW UNDER **BLACK,** a CARD --

SATURDAY

The rapping, at first tentative and polite, grows insistent. Then we hear someone get out of bed.

> MILES (O.S.)
> ...the fuck...

A DOOR is opened, and the black gives way to BLINDING WHITE LIGHT, the way one experiences the first glimpse of day amid, say, a hangover.

A WORKER is there.

> MILES (O.S.) (CONT'D)
> Yeah?

> WORKER
> Hi, Miles. Can you move your car, please?

> MILES (O.S.)
> Why?

> WORKER
> The painters got to put the truck in, and you didn't park too good.

> MILES (O.S.)
> (a sigh, then --)
> Yeah, hold on.

He closes the door with a SLAM.

EXT. MILES'S APARTMENT COMPLEX - DAY

SUPERIMPOSE --

SAN DIEGO, CALIFORNIA

Wearing only underwear, a bathrobe and clogs, MILES RAYMOND comes out of his unit and heads toward the street. He passes some SIX MEXICANS waiting to work.

He climbs into his twelve-year-old CONVERTIBLE SAAB, parked far from the curb and blocking part of the driveway. The car starts fitfully.

As he pulls away, the guys begin backing up the truck.

3   **EXT. STREET - DAY**   3

Miles rounds the corner and finds a new parking spot.

4   **INT. CAR - CONTINUOUS**   4

He cuts the engine, exhales a long breath and brings his
hands to his head in a gesture of headache pain or just
anguish. He leans back in his seat, closes his eyes, and
soon NODS OFF.

5   **INT. MILES'S APARTMENT - DAY**   5

The door bursts open. Miles runs into the kitchen,
looking just past camera.

                         MILES
              Fuck!

WHIP PAN to --

THE MICROWAVE CLOCK that reads 10:50.

ON THE PHONE --

Miles hurriedly throws clothes into a suitcase.

                         MILES (CONT'D)
              Yeah, no, I know I said I'd be there by
              noon, but there's been all this work going
              on at my building, and it's like a total
              nightmare, and I had a bunch of stuff to
              deal with this morning. But I'm on my
              way. I'm out the door right this second.
              It's going to be great. Yeah. Bye.

6   **INT. MILES'S BATHROOM - DAY**   6

ON THE TOILET --

Miles has a BOOK propped open on his knees. He turns a
page, lost in his reading.

LATER --

Miles SHOWERS.

IN THE MIRROR --

Miles FLOSSES.

INT. COFFEE HOUSE - DAY   7

Miles finally makes it to the front of the line.

> BARISTA
> Hey, Miles.

> MILES
> Hey, Simon. Triple espresso, please.

> BARISTA
> Rough night, huh?
> (ringing it up)
> For here?

> MILES
> No, I'm running late. Make it to go.
> And give me a New York Times and...
> (scanning the display case)
> ...a spinach croissant.

EXT. 5 FREEWAY ENTRANCE RAMP - DAY   8

Miles's Saab chugs up the ramp and merges.

INSERT - NEW YORK TIMES CROSSWORD PUZZLE --   9

-- pressed against the STEERING WHEEL. The puzzle is
about 1/3 finished.

EXT. 5 FREEWAY - DAY   10

As though from an adjacent car, we see Miles driving
while carefully filling in an answer.

INT./EXT. SAAB - DAY   11

THROUGH THE WINDSHIELD --

A SIGN reads:

> RANCHO PALOS VERDES
> PALOS VERDES ESTATES
> 1/4 MILE

PAN TO MILES as he signals to change lanes. The finished puzzle lies on the passenger seat.

12   **EXT. PALOS VERDES STREET - DAY**   12

The houses on this block are blandly palatial as in so many affluent Southern California suburbs.

Miles's car pulls into the driveway behind an older BMW and two LEXI. He gets out and trots toward the front door.

13   **INT. ERGANIAN HOUSE - DAY**   13

A GIANT PROJECTION TV --
in a large split-level living room displays a GOLF TOURNAMENT.

WIDE --

Watching from the ultra-comfortable furniture are MIKE ERGANIAN, a tanned, silver-haired real estate *caudillo*; bride-to-be CHRISTINE ERGANIAN, his oldest daughter; and JACK LOPATE, wearing bowling shirt, shorts and flip-flops.

MRS. ERGANIAN, a warm and elegant housewife, shows Miles into the room.

                    MRS. ERGANIAN
          Look what the cat dragged!

                    MILES
          Hi, everybody.

Mr. Erganian and Jack get to their feet and shake hands with Miles. Jack remains affable, but we can discern his genuine irritation.

                    JACK
          About time you got here, bud. Mr.
          Prompt.

                    MR. ERGANIAN
          We were thinking maybe you took the wrong
          way and went to Tijuana and they didn't
          let you back in.

The Erganians laugh. Miles works up a smile too.

                    MILES
          I had to bribe them.

More lame laughter.

                    CHRISTINE
          Hey, Miles.

                    MILES
               (leaning to kiss Christine)
          Seriously though, the freeway was
          unbelievable today. Unbelievable. Bumper
          to bumper the whole way. People getting
          an early start on the weekend, I guess.
          Granted I got a late start, but still.

Although Mr. Erganian presses MUTE on the remote, he keeps
watching for an extended moment, as do Jack and Miles.

                    MRS. ERGANIAN
          Christine, why don't you ask Miles about
          the cake?

                    CHRISTINE
          Oh, good idea. Here, Miles, come to the
          kitchen with me.

                    JACK
          Don't bother him with that. We got to
          get going.

                    CHRISTINE
               (taking Miles's hand)
          It'll just take a second.

INT. ERGANIAN KITCHEN - DAY   14

Jack and the Erganians surround Miles as he eats from a
plate with two pieces of CAKE -- one white, one dark.

                    MRS. ERGANIAN
          Jack tells us you are publishing a book.
          Congratulations.

                    MR. ERGANIAN
          Yes, congratulations.

Miles shoots Jack a look. Mr. Erganian gets some ice
cubes from the refrigerator door.

                    MILES
          Yeah, well, it's not exactly finalized
          yet, but, um, there has been some
          interest and --

                              MRS. ERGANIAN
                         (to Jack)
                    Your friend is modest.

                              JACK
                    Yeah, Miles, don't be so modest. Indulge
                    them. Don't make me out a liar.

                              MR. ERGANIAN
                    What subject is your book? Non-fiction?

                              MILES
                    No, it's a novel. Fiction. Although
                    there's a lot from my own life, so I
                    guess technically some of it is non-
                    fiction.

                              MR. ERGANIAN
                    Good. I like non-fiction. There is so
                    much to know about the world that I think
                    reading a story someone just invented is
                    kind of a waste of time.

                              CHRISTINE
                    So which one do you like better?

                              MILES
                    I like them both, but if pressed I'd have
                    to say I prefer the dark.

                              JACK
                         (to Christine)
                    See?

15   **INT. SAAB - CONTINUOUS**   15

IN A REAR VIEW MIRROR --

The Erganians wave good-bye.

INSIDE THE CAR --

Miles accelerates as he and Jack wave back.

                              JACK
                    Where the fuck were you, man? I was
                    dying in there. We were supposed to be a
                    hundred miles away by now.

                              MILES
                    I can't help the traffic.

                         JACK
          Come on. You're fucking hungover.

                         MILES
          Okay, there was a tasting last night.
          But I wanted to get us some stuff for the
          ride up. Check out the box.

Jack turns around, and starts rooting around in a
CARDBOARD WINE BOX.

                         MILES (CONT'D)
          Why did you tell them my book was being published?

                         JACK
          You said you had it all lined up.

                         MILES
          No, I didn't. What I *said* was that my agent had
          heard there was some interest at Conundrum...

                         JACK
          Yeah, Conundrum.

                         MILES
          ...and that one of the editors was passing
          it up to a senior editor. She was supposed
          to hear something this week, but now it's
          next week, and... It's always like this.
          It's always a fucking waiting game. I've
          been through it too many times already.   *

                         JACK
          I don't know. Senior Editor? Sounds
          like you're in to me.

                         MILES
          It's a long-shot, all right? And Conundrum
          is just a small specialty press anyway. I'm   *
          not getting my hopes up. I've stopped   *
          caring. That's it. I've stopped caring.   *

Jack sits back in his seat holding a bottle of CHAMPAGNE
and TWO GLASSES.

                         JACK
          But I know it's going to happen this
          time. I can feel it. This is the one.
          I'm proud of you, man. You're the
          smartest guy I know.

Jack now begins to remove the foil from the champagne
bottle.

                        MILES
          Don't open that now. It's warm.

                        JACK
          Come on, we're celebrating. I say we pop
          it.

                        MILES
          That's a 1992 Byron. It's really rare.
          Don't open it now. I've been saving it!

Jack untwists the wire. Instantly the cork pops off, and
a fountain of champagne erupts.

                        MILES (CONT'D)
          For Christ's sake, Jack! You just wasted
          like half of it!

Jack beings pouring two glasses.

                        JACK
          Shut up.
                    (handing Miles a glass)
          Here's to a great week.

                        MILES
                    (coming around)
          Yes. Absolutely. Despite your crass
          behavior, I'm really glad we're finally
          getting this time together.

                        JACK
          Yeah.

                        MILES
          You know how long I've been begging to
          take you on the wine tour. I was
          beginning to think it was never going to
          happen.

They clink and drink.

                        JACK
          Oh, that's tasty.

                        MILES
          100% Pinot Noir. Single vineyard. They
          don't even make it anymore.

                        JACK
          Pinot Noir? How come it's white?
          Doesn't noir mean dark?

          MILES
Jesus. Don't ask questions like that up
in the wine country. They'll think
you're a moron.

          JACK
Just tell me.

          MILES
Color in red wines comes from the skins.
This juice is free run, so there's no
skin contact in the fermentation, ergo no
color.

          JACK
      (not really listening)
Sure is tasty.

EXT. FREEWAY - DAY   16

The Saab heads north.

INT. SAAB - DAY   17

The boys continue to drink and drive.

          MILES
Did you read the latest draft, by the way?

          JACK
Oh yeah. Yeah.

          MILES
And?

          JACK
I liked it a lot. A lot of improvements.
It just seemed overall, I don't know,
tighter, more... congealed or something.

          MILES
How about the new ending? Did you like
that?

          JACK
Oh yeah. Much better.

          MILES
There is no new ending. Page 750 on is
exactly the same.

                         JACK
               Well, then I guess it must have felt new
               because everything leading up to it was
               so different.

17A   **EXT. GAS STATION #1 - DAY**   17A

Miles is pumping gas. Jack is stretching his legs nearby
or perhaps cleaning the windshield.

A CELLPHONE RINGS. Jack reaches into his pocket.

                         JACK
                    (looking at the phone)
               It's Christine.
                    (snapping it open)
               Hey you.

                         CHRISTINE (ON PHONE)
               You guys having fun?

Christine's voice is so loud that Jack has to hold the
phone away from his ear.

                         JACK
               Yeah. All twenty minutes so far have
               been a blast.

                         CHRISTINE (ON THE PHONE)
               Good. That's good.

A silence, then --

                         JACK
               So what's up?

                         CHRISTINE (ON THE PHONE)
               Just seeing how you're doing. And, um,
               Mom and I were starting to look over the
               seating charts again, and we're wondering
               if you wanted Tony Levin to sit next to
               the Feldmans, or should he be at one of
               the singles tables?

Jack looks at Miles in a mute appeal for sympathy.

                         CHRISTINE (ON THE PHONE)
                         (CONT'D)
               So what do you think? With the Feldmans?

Jack hasn't even really heard the question.

                    JACK
          Yeah, the Feldmans.

As the conversation continues, Miles replaces the GAS
PUMP, screws the GAS CAP back on, and together the guys
get back into the car. We DRIVE AWAY WITH THEM.

               CHRISTINE (ON THE PHONE)
          Really? Because I don't know, I was
          thinking that --

                    JACK
          Well, then put him at the singles table.

               CHRISTINE (ON THE PHONE)
          The problem with that is that then
          there's one extra --

                    JACK
          Then put him with the Feldmans. Whatever
          you and your Mom decide is fine with me.

               CHRISTINE (ON THE PHONE)
          Don't dismiss me. I'm trying to include
          you in this decision. He's <u>your</u> friend.

                    JACK
          I didn't dismiss you. I told you what I
          thought, but it didn't seem to matter, so you
          decide. Besides, this is supposed to be my
          time with Miles. I hope you're not going to
          call every five minutes.

               CHRISTINE (ON THE PHONE)
          I'm not going to call every five minutes,
          but this is important.

                    JACK
          Honey, I'm just saying you know I need a
          little space before the wedding. Isn't
          that the point of this? Isn't that what
          we talked about with Dr. Gertler?

A silence. Then --

               CHRISTINE (ON THE PHONE)
          Why are you being so defensive?

                    JACK
          I don't know, Christine. Perhaps it's
          because I feel attacked.

>   CHRISTINE (ON THE PHONE)
>   I ask you one simple question, and
>   suddenly I'm attacking you.
>
>   JACK
>   Listen. I'll call you when we get there,
>   and we can talk about it then, okay?
>   Okay?
>
>   CHRISTINE (ON THE PHONE)
>   Bye.
>
>   JACK
>   I love you.
>
>   CHRISTINE (ON THE PHONE)
>   Bye.

Jack SLAMS his cellphone shut, momentarily blinded with
rage.

>   MILES
>   Tony Levin? Why did you fucking invite
>   Tony Levin?

18   **EXT. 405 FREEWAY - LATE AFTERNOON**   18

The Saab heads north -- now passing through LOS ANGELES.

19   **INT./EXT. SAAB - LATE AFTERNOON**   19

Miles signals and begins to head for an EXIT.

>   JACK
>   Whoa, why are we getting off?
>
>   MILES
>   I've just got to make one quick stop.
>   Won't take a second.
>
>   JACK
>   What?
>
>   MILES
>   I thought we could just say a quick hello
>   to my mother.
>
>   JACK
>   Your mother? Jesus, Miles, we were
>   supposed to be up there hours ago.

                    MILES
          It's her birthday tomorrow. And I don't
          feel right driving by her house and not
          stopping in, okay? It'll just take a
          second. She's right off the freeway.

EXT. 101 FREEWAY - LATE AFTERNOON   20

The Saab takes an EXIT.

                    JACK (O.S.
          How old's she going to be?

                    MILES (O.S.)
          Um... seventy... something.

                    JACK (O.S.)
          That's a good age.

OMIT   21

OMIT   22

EXT. CONDO COMMUNITY STREET - DUSK   23

The Saab rounds a corner and parks in front of a modest CONDO.

SUPERIMPOSE:

                    OXNARD, CALIFORNIA

EXT. MILES'S MOTHER'S CONDO - DUSK   24

Approaching the front door, Miles pulls a BOUQUET OF
FLOWERS out of a plastic grocery store bag. Jack carries
a bottle of CHAMPAGNE.

Miles pulls a BIRTHDAY CARD out of the bag too.

                    MILES
          Wait a second.

He pulls a PEN from his pocket and signs it. As he licks
the envelope, Jack rings the bell.

Moments later PHYLLIS comes to the door. She is a matronly older woman in a nightgown and housecoat.

> MILES AND JACK
> Surprise! Happy birthday!

The boys offer up the flowers and champagne. Phyllis slurs slightly as she speaks -- she's been doing some celebrating of her own.

> PHYLLIS
> My God. Miles. And Jack! What a surprise. I can't remember the last time you brought me flowers.

They hug.

> JACK
> They're from both of us.

> PHYLLIS
> A famous actor bringing me flowers on my birthday. Don't I feel special?

> MILES
> A famous actor who's getting married next week.

> PHYLLIS
> Oh, that's right. Isn't that nice? I hope that girl knows how lucky she is, marrying no less than Derek Summersby.

The boys follow her inside.

25   **INT. MILES'S MOTHER'S CONDO - CONTINUOUS**   25

> JACK
> Jeez, Mrs. Raymond, that was eleven years ago.

> PHYLLIS
> Well, you were wonderful on that show. I never understood why they had to give you that brain tumor so soon. Why that didn't make you the biggest movie star in the world is a sin. It's a sin.

> JACK
> Yeah, well, you should be my agent.

                    PHYLLIS
         If I was, I would sing your praises up and
         down the street until they put me in the
         loony bin. Now Miles, why didn't you tell
         me you were coming and bringing this
         handsome man? Look how I'm dressed. I've
         got to run and put my face on.

                    JACK
         You look fabulous, Mrs. Raymond.

                    PHYLLIS
              (over her shoulder)
         Oh, stop it. Make yourselves comfortable.
              (now around the corner)
         You boys hungry?

                    MILES
         Yeah, I'm hungry.

Jack gives Miles a look.

                    MILES (CONT'D)
              (low)
         Just a snack. Calm down.

Miles leads Jack into this small condo. The TV is on,
and it's MESSY. Amid the newspapers and junk mail and
dishes, an AB-ROLLER and an ancient SCHWINN EXER-CYCLE
sit forgotten in a corner.

INT. MILES'S MOTHER'S KITCHEN - NIGHT   26

Miles finishes twisting ice trays into a MOP BUCKET as it
fills with water in the sink. He puts the champagne in
and carries it into the --

INT. MILES'S MOTHER'S LIVING ROOM - CONTINUOUS   27

He takes a seat on the sofa next to Jack, who is watching
WHO WANTS TO BE A MILLIONAIRE?

                    MILES
         Let me show you something. The secret to
         opening champagne is that once the cork
         is released, you keep pressure on it so
         you don't --

                    JACK
              (concentrated on the TV)
         Just a second. Guy's going for $2500.

Miles finishes opening the bottle with an elegant silence.

> PHYLLIS (O.S.)
> Ready for my close up!

The boys turn to see Phyllis now dolled up in thick make-up and a PANTSUIT. Her eyebrows are painted and cock-eyed. Overall she looks much worse than before.

> PHYLLIS (CONT'D)
> Oh, champagne! Miles, why don't you
> bring that out onto the lanai? I thought
> we could eat on the lanai.

28   **EXT. MILES'S MOTHER'S LANAI - NIGHT**   28

Miles and Jack are seated in webbed chairs around a circular glass table. They are mid-meal. Everyone is more than a little lubricated, especially the birthday girl as she returns from the kitchen with another plate of food.

> JACK
> Mrs. Raymond, this is delicious.
> Absolutely delicious.

> PHYLLIS
> (sitting)
> They're just leftovers.

> JACK
> Is it chicken?

> PHYLLIS
> I could have made something fancier if a
> certain someone had let me know that a
> certain someone was coming for a visit
> with a certain special friend. Could
> have made a pork roast.

> MILES
> It was a surprise, Mom.

> PHYLLIS
> And I could have already put clean sheets
> on the other bed and the fold-out. You
> are staying. Wendy, Ron and the twins
> are picking us up at 11:30 to go to
> brunch at the Sheraton. They do a
> magnificent job there. Wendy is so
> excited you're coming.

Silence. Jack freezes, his fork halfway to his mouth.

                    MILES
          You talked to Wendy?

                    PHYLLIS
          Just now. She's thrilled. And the kids.

                    MILES
               (trying to be chipper)
          Yeah, well. You know, Jack's pretty
          eager to get up to... you know, but, uh,
          yeah. We'll see how it goes.

                    PHYLLIS
          Well, you boys do what you want. I just
          think it would be nice for us to be
          together as a family on my birthday.

                    MILES
          Uh-huh.
               (wiping his mouth)
          I'll be right back.

He gets up and heads into the house.

INT. MILES'S MOTHER'S HALLWAY - NIGHT   29

Miles heads toward...

INT. MILES'S MOTHER'S BEDROOM - NIGHT   30

... and goes directly to her dresser, opening a drawer
filled with bras, panties and stockings.

He burrows through his mother's lingerie until locating a
CAN OF RAID. A can of Raid?

He twists open the bottom and pulls it apart, revealing
it to be a SECRET STASH for valuables disguised as a
common household product. Inside are stacks of ONE-
HUNDRED DOLLAR BILLS.

                    MILES
               (quickly peeling some off)
          ... six, seven, eight,...
               (one more for good luck)
          Nine.

His task complete, he closes the drawer, and as he stuffs the bills in his pocket, his glance falls upon FRAMED PHOTOS atop the dresser --

-- A proud NINE-YEAR-OLD MILES poses in front of his childhood San Diego home, showing off a WAGON filled with freshly harvested lettuce. On the wagon is a hand-lettered sign -- "10 cents a bunch."

-- A Sears portrait shows the RAYMOND FAMILY: a much younger Phyllis, her husband, and their two children -- a 12-year-old Miles and seven-year-old Wendy.

-- Miles at his wedding. He and his bride VICTORIA look young and attractive, their faces radiant and hopeful.

31   **INT. MILES'S MOTHER'S BATHROOM - NIGHT**   31

Miles enters, FLUSHES the toilet and leaves.

32   **EXT. MILES'S MOTHER'S LANAI - NIGHT**   32

As Miles slides open the door and takes his seat again, Jack is pouring Phyllis another glass.

>   PHYLLIS
> And what was that other one you did, the
> one where you're the jogger?

>   JACK
> Oh, that was for, uh, wait... That was
> for Spray and Wash.

>   PHYLLIS
> Spray and Wash. That's the one.

>   JACK
> Yeah, I remember the girl who was in it
> with me. She was something.

>   PHYLLIS
> I just remember you jogging. So when's
> the wedding?

>   MILES
>   (irritated)
> This Saturday, Mom, remember? We told
> you.

> JACK
> And Miles is my best man, Mrs. Raymond.
> My main man.

> PHYLLIS
> (another drink of wine)
> Miles, when are you going to get married
> again?

> MILES
> I just got divorced. Phyllis.

> JACK
> Two years ago, buddy.

> PHYLLIS
> You should get back together with
> Victoria. She was good for you.

Embarrassed for his friend, Jack just stares at his food.

> PHYLLIS (CONT'D)
> She was good for you.
> (turning to Jack)
> And so beautiful and intelligent. You
> knew her, right?

> JACK
> Oh, yeah. Real well. Still do.

> PHYLLIS
> I'm worried about you, Miles. Do you
> need some money?

> MILES
> I'm fine.

Miles takes another drink of wine.

CUT TO BLACK

UNDER BLACK, a CARD --

SUNDAY

> MILES (O.S.)
> Jack. Jack.

INT. MILES'S MOTHER'S BEDROOM - DAY   33

Jack finally awakens with a start and finds Miles
standing above him, shaking him.

WIDE --

As Jack gets up, we see he has crashed on Phyllis's bed adorned with all her decorative PILLOWS.

34   **INT. MILES'S MOTHER'S LIVING ROOM - DAY**   34

Still in her pantsuit and smeared makeup, Phyllis lies sprawled and snoring on the sofa. On the TV, ostensibly never turned off the night before, is an inane CARTOON.

As Miles opens the front door, he spots Jack heading toward the TV to turn it off. Miles waves him off.

> MILES
> (a loud whisper)
> She'll wake up.

As they leave and Miles closes the front door quietly behind him, we PAN to the flowers still wrapped and forgotten on a side table.

35   **INT. ROADSIDE IHOP - DAY**   35

TWO PLATES OF FOOD
float in front of two breasts tucked inside a zippered uniform.

WIDER --

Disheveled and unshaven, Jack and Miles are served breakfast by a young, innocently sexy WAITRESS. Jack leers after her.

> JACK
> Fuck, man. Too early in the morning for that, you know what I mean?

> MILES
> She's a kid, Jack. I don't even look at that stuff anymore.

> JACK
> That's your problem, Miles.

> MILES
> As if she'd even be attracted to guys like us/ in the first place.

                    JACK
          Speak for yourself. I get chicks looking
          at me all the time. All ages.

                    MILES
          It's not worth it. You pay too big a
          price. It's never free.

They eat in silence a moment.

                    JACK
          You need to get laid.

Miles shrugs off the comment.

                    JACK (CONT'D)
          It'd be the best thing for you. You know
          what? I'm going to get you laid this
          week. That's going to be my best man
          gift to you. I'm not going to give you a
          pen knife or a gift certificate or any of
          that other horseshit.

                    MILES
          I'd rather have a knife.

                    JACK
          No. No. You've been officially depressed
          for like two years now, and you were always
          a negative guy anyway, even in college. Now
          it's worse -- you're wasting away. Teaching
          English to fucking eighth-graders when they
          should be reading what you wrote. Your
          books.

                    MILES
          I'm working on it.

Miles concentrates on his eggs and hash browns.

                    JACK
          You still seeing that shrink?

                    MILES
          I went on Monday. But I spent most of
          the time helping him with his computer.

                    JACK
          Well, I say fuck therapy and what's that
          stuff you take, Xanax?

                    MILES
          And Lexapro, yes.

                         JACK
          Well, I say fuck that. You need to get
          your joint worked on, that's what you
          need.

                         MILES
          Jack. This week is not about me. It's
          about you. I'm going to show you a good
          time. We're going to drink a lot of good
          wine, play some golf, eat some great
          food, enjoy the scenery and send you off
          in style.

                         JACK
          And get your bone smooched.

Jack spots the waitress coming out of the kitchen and
motions for more coffee. She nods and smiles, indicating
she'll be right over. Jack returns the smile and holds
up a hand to signal he'll wait. Jack turns back to see
Miles watching him.

                         JACK (CONT'D)
          What?

36   **EXT. CENTRAL COAST - DAY**   36

In a series of shots, the Saab -- now with its TOP DOWN --
makes its way onto the 101 and travels past landmarks
that those familiar with the Santa Barbara area might
recognize.

MUSIC accompanies this sequence that anchors us into the
rhythm of a road trip.

37   **INT./EXT SAAB - DAY**   37

The car now descends the Santa Ynez Mountains and heads
toward Buellton. Miles and Jack must SHOUT to be heard
in the open car.

                         MILES
          You know what? Let's take the Santa Rosa
          turnoff and hit Sanford first.

                         JACK
          Whatever's closest, man. I need a glass.

                         MILES
          These guys make top-notch Pinot and
          Chardonnay.
                         (MORE)

                    MILES (CONT'D)
One of the best producers in Santa
Barbara county.
          (looking out the window)
Look how beautiful this view is. What a
day!

                    JACK
I thought you hated Chardonnay.

                    MILES
I like all varietals. I just don't
generally like the way they manipulate
Chardonnay in California -- too much oak
and secondary malolactic fermentation.

Jacks nods without any idea what Miles is talking about.

EXT. SANTA ROSA TURN-OFF - DAY   38

The Saab passes over the 101 and turns onto SANTA ROSA road.

INT./EXT. SAAB - DAY   39

The boys now pass vineyards of immaculate grapevines.

                    MILES
Jesus, _what a day_! Isn't it gorgeous?
And the ocean's just right over that
ridge. See, the reason this region's
great for Pinot is that the cold air off
the Pacific flows in at night through
these transverse valleys and cools down
the berries. Pinot's a very thin-skinned
grape and doesn't like heat or humidity.

Jack looks at Miles, admiring his friend's vast learning
and articulateness.

The Saab now pulls off the road and makes its way down a
long gravel DRIVEWAY.

                    JACK
Hey, Miles. I really hope your novel
sells.

                    MILES
Thanks, Jack. So do I.
          (noticing)
Here we are.

40   **EXT. SANFORD TASTING ROOM - DAY**   40

Miles brings the car to a stop in the parking lot. As
they get out and walk --

                    MILES
          So what'd you guys finally decide on for
          the menu?

                    JACK
          I told you. Filet and salmon.

                    MILES
          Yeah, but how are they making the salmon?
          Poached with a yogurt-dill sauce?
          Teriyaki? Curry?

                    JACK
          I don't know. Salmon. Don't you always
          have white wine with fish?

                    MILES
          Oh, Jesus. Look, at some point we have
          to find out because it's going to make a
          big difference.

                    JACK
               (taking out his phone)
          Let me call Christine.

                    MILES
          Doesn't have to be now. Let's go taste.

                    JACK
          I owe her a call anyway.

Miles must curb his eagerness to go inside the tasting
room as Jack SPEED DIALS.

                    JACK (CONT'D)
          Hey, honey. So we're up here about to
          taste some whites, and we need to know how
          the caterers are going to make the salmon.

Jack listens, then grows suddenly impatient.

                    JACK (CONT'D)
          No, I know, I didn't forget, but we wound up at
          Miles's mom's house, and it got really late,
          and it was hard to call, so I'm calling you
          now. I said I was sorry. Yes, I did.
               (MORE)

>   JACK (CONT'D)
>   (to Miles)
>   You heard me say I was sorry, right?

Miles just shrugs.

>   JACK (CONT'D)
>   Miles heard me say I was sorry.

As Jack gets more and more involved with the phone call, he
wanders off across the parking lot, progressively out of earshot.

>   JACK (CONT'D)
>   Give me a break, will you? I just called to find
>   out about the salmon -- for our wedding -- to be
>   more involved, like you said -- and all you want
>   to do is get into it about last night and, okay,
>   I'm sorry. I'm sorry I didn't call. You're
>   totally right. I know, but I'm trying to make
>   this the best wedding I can with the best wine we
>   can find. Don't I get any credit for that? Okay.
>   Look, I've got to go. I'm out here in the parking
>   lot, and Miles is waiting for me...

And so it goes, Jack's voice rising and falling. Miles
decides to head inside.

INT. SANFORD TASTING ROOM - DAY   41

Miles is at the bar, TWO GLASSES in front of him. Jack
walks in and bellies up next to him.

>   JACK
>   (proudly)
>   Baked with a butter-lime glaze.

>   MILES
>   Now we're talking.

CHRIS BURROUGHS, a POURER in a cowboy hat and ponytail,
comes over.

>   CHRIS
>   This the condemned man?

>   MILES
>   Here he is. Jack, Chris. Chris, Jack.

Chris and Jack shake hands.

>   JACK
>   How you doing?

                         CHRIS
          You guys want to start with the Vin Gris?

                         JACK
          Sounds good.

TWO GLASSES are filled with small amounts of PINOT NOIR
VIN GRIS.

                         JACK (CONT'D)
          This is rosé, right?

                         MILES
          Good, yeah, it is a rosé. Only this one
          is rather atypically made from 100% Pinot
          Noir.

                         JACK
          Pinot noir? Not again!
               (joking, to Chris)
          You know, not all Pinots are noir.

They laugh.

Miles swirls his glass in tight circles on the bar, then
lifts it to smell. Jack clumsily imitates Miles, perhaps
even spilling some wine in the process.

                         MILES
          Let me show you.

We see details of what Miles now describes.

                         MILES (CONT'D)
          First take your glass and examine the wine
          against the light. You're looking at color
          and clarity.

                         JACK
          What color is it supposed to be?

                         MILES
          Depends on the varietal. Just get a
          sense of it. Thick? Thin? Watery?
          Syrupy? Inky? Amber, whatever..

                         JACK
          Huh.

                         MILES
          Now tip it. What you're doing here is
          checking for color density as it thins
          toward the rim.
                         (MORE)

                    MILES (CONT'D)
          Tells you how old it is, among other
          things, usually more important with reds.
          This is a very young wine, so it's going
          to retain its color pretty solidly. Now
          stick your nose in it.

Jack waves the glass under his nose as if it were a
perfume bottle.

                    MILES (CONT'D)
          Don't be shy. Get your nose in there.

Jack now buries his nose in the glass.

                    MILES (CONT'D)
          What do you smell?

                    JACK
          I don't know. Wine? Fermented grapes?

Miles smells.

                    MILES
          There's not much there yet, but you can
          still find...
                    (more sniffs)
          ... a little citrus... maybe some
          strawberry... passion fruit... and
          there's even a hint of like asparagus...
          or like a nutty Edam cheese.

Jack smells again and begins to brighten.

                    JACK
          Huh. Maybe a little strawberry. Yeah,
          strawberry. I'm not so sure about the
          cheese.

                    MILES
          Now set your glass down and get some air
          into it.

Miles expertly swirls the wine. Jacks follows suit.

                    MILES (CONT'D)
          Oxygenating it opens it up, unlocks the
          aroma and the flavors. Very important.
          Now we smell again.

They do so. Jack smiles.

                    MILES (CONT'D)
          That's what you do with every one.

                         JACK
          When do we get to drink it?

                         MILES
             Now.

Jack gulps his wine down in one shot. Miles chews his
before swallowing.

                         JACK
          So how would you rate this one?

                         MILES
          Usually they start you on the wines with
          learning disabilities, but this one's
          pretty damn good.
                    (to Chris)
          This is the new one, right, Chris?

                         CHRIS
          Released it about two months ago.

                         MILES
             Nice job.

                         CHRIS
             We like it.

                         JACK
                    (to Miles)
          You know, you could work in a wine store.

                         MILES
          Yeah, that would be a good move.

Now Miles notices something about Jack.

                         MILES (CONT'D)
          Are you chewing gum?

                         JACK
             Want some?

41A   **EXT. SOLVANG, CALIFORNIA - DAY**   41A

        The Saab passes through this Danish-themed tourist town.

        SUPERIMPOSE --

                         SOLVANG

EXT. BUELLTON, CALIFORNIA -- DAY   42

The Saab makes its way into this very average-looking
Central Coast town right off the freeway.

SUPERIMPOSE --
                        BUELLTON

EXT. WINDMILL INN - DAY   43

The Saab pulls into the parking lot of this motel. And
look -- there's the WINDMILL itself, its decorative
blades motionless.

INT. MOTEL ROOM - DAY   44

Miles and Jack enter the room and throw their suitcases
onto their respective beds.

LATER --

The sounds of a SHOWER and OFF-KEY SINGING come from the
bathroom while Miles sits impatiently on the bed. He
pounds on the wall.

                        MILES
            Hey Jack, hurry up!

                        JACK (O.S.)
            Just a minute!

Opening the bedside drawer, Miles finds a GIDEON'S BIBLE
and tosses it in the trash -- apparently his hotel
routine.

EXT. HIGHWAY 246 - DUSK   45

Freshly showered and dressed for dinner, Miles and Jack
amble along the shoulder of this busy local two-lane
highway. They pass a mall and a car dealership.

                        JACK
            I thought you said it was close. Now I'm
            all pitted out.

                        MILES
            It's not even a mile.

                    JACK
We should have driven.

                    MILES
Not with the wine list these people have.
We don't want to hold back.

                    JACK
You think I'm making a mistake marrying
Christine?

                    MILES
Whoa.

                    JACK
Come on, do you think I'm doing the right
thing? Tell the truth. You've been
through it.

                    MILES
Well, you waited for some good reason,
and you proposed to Christine for some
good reason. So I think it's great.
It's time. You've got to have your eyes
open, that's all. I mean, look at me. I
thought Victoria and I were set for life.

                    JACK
Christine's dad -- he's been talking about
bringing me into his property business.
Showing me the ropes. And that's something,
considering how long it took him to get over
I'm not Armenian. So I'm thinking about it.
But I don't know, might get a little
incestuous. But Mike does pretty well. A
lot of high-end commercial stuff.

                    MILES
So you're going to stop acting?

                    JACK
No way. This would just provide some
stability is what I'm saying. I can always
squeeze in an audition or a commercial here
and there, you know, keep myself in the
game in case something big comes along.

                    MILES
Uh-huh.

                    JACK
         We're not getting any younger, right? And
         my career, well, it's gotten pretty, you
         know, frustrating. Even with my new
         manager. Maybe it's time to settle down.

                    MILES
         If that's what feels right.

                    JACK
              (convincing himself)
         It does. Feels right.

                    MILES
         Then it's a good thing.

                    JACK
              (nodding, feeling better)
         Yeah. It's good. Feels good.

Miles leads them away from the road and across a parking
lot. The camera PANS to reveal --

THE HITCHING POST,
a local institution.

INT. HITCHING POST BAR - DUSK   46

Miles and Jack belly up. GARY, the Samoan bartender,
spots Miles and extends a welcoming hand.

                    GARY
         Hey, Miles. Long time no see.

                    MILES
         Gary.

                    GARY
         When's that novel of yours coming out?
         We all want to read it.

                    MILES
         Soon, soon. Say, this is my buddy Jack.
         He's getting married next week.

                    GARY
              (shaking Jack's hand)
         My condolences.

                    MILES
         What are you pouring tonight?

                    GARY
          Lot of good stuff.
               (looking at a row of bottles)
          Got the new Bien Nacido. Want a taste?

                    MILES
          Absolutement.
               (to Jack)
          They have their own label that's just
          outstanding.

Gary pours Jack and Miles a generous sample and the two
men swirl, sniff and taste. Jack is beginning to get the
hang of things.

                    GARY
          What do you think?

                    MILES
          Tight as a nun's asshole but good
          concentration. Nice fruit.

                    JACK
          Yeah. Tight.

                    MILES
               (to Gary)
          Pour us a couple.

Gary fills their glasses and corks the bottle. Jack
raises his glass to toast.

                    JACK
          Here's to my last week of freedom.

                    MILES
          It's going to be great. Here's to us.

They clink their glasses and take a drink. We linger on
them as Miles retreats inward and a restless Jack scans
the room.

47   **INT. HITCHING POST DINING ROOM - NIGHT**   47

Jack and Miles review their menus. Jack looks up and
spots a PRETTY WAITRESS placing an order at the bar.

                    JACK
          Miles. Check it out.

Miles glances at the waitress and returns to his menu.

                    MILES
          Oh, yeah. That's Maya.

                    JACK
          You know her?

                    MILES
          Sure I know Maya.

                    JACK
          You *know* that chick?

                    MILES
          Jack, this is where I eat when I come up
          here. It's practically my office. And
          sometimes I have a drink with the
          employees. Maya's great. She's worked
          here about a year, maybe a year and a half.

                    JACK
          She is very hot.

                    MILES
          And very nice. And very married. Check
          out the rock.

Jack leans forward and squints.

                    JACK
          Doesn't mean shit. When Christine was a
          hostess at Sushi Roku, she wore a big
          engagement ring to keep guys from hitting
          on her. Think it worked? Fuck no. How
          do you think I met her?

                    MILES
          This gal's married to I think a
          Philosophy professor at UC Santa Barbara.

                    JACK
          So what's a professor's wife doing
          waitressing? Obviously that's over.

                    MILES
          You don't know anything about this woman.
          Calm down. Let's just eat, okay?
                    (focusing on the menu)
          The duck is excellent and pairs nicely
          with the Highliner Pinot.

Just then Maya comes by carrying a tray of food on her
way to another table.

                         MAYA
          Hey, Miles. Good to see you.

                         MILES
          Maya, how are you?

                         MAYA
          I'm doing good, good. You look great.
          Did you lose some weight?

                         MILES
          Uh, no, actually. Busy night.

                         MAYA
          Oh yeah, Sunday night. You guys been out
          tasting today?

                         MILES
          You know it. This is my friend Jack.
          Jack, Maya.

                         JACK
               (big smile)
          Hiya.

                         MAYA
               (smiling back)
          Hi. Well, nice to see you guys here.
          Bye, Miles.

She goes.

                         JACK
          Jesus, she's jammin'. And she likes you.
          What else do you know about her?

                         MILES
          Well, she does know a lot about wine.

                         JACK
          Oooooohh. Now we're getting somewhere.

                         MILES
          And she likes Pinot.

                         JACK
          Perfect.

                         MILES
          Jack, she's a fucking waitress in
          Buellton. How would that ever work?

                    JACK
          Why do you always focus on the negative?
          Didn't you see how friendly she was to
          you?

                    MILES
          She works for tips!

                    JACK
          You're blind, dude. Blind.

Miles focuses again on the menu.

                    MILES
          I also recommend the ostrich. Very lean.
          Locally raised.

8   **INT. HITCHING POST BAR - NIGHT**   48

TWO BURGUNDY GLASSES --

are refilled with the contents of yet another bottle of
Hitching Post Pinot Noir.

WIDE --

Jack and Miles are enjoying a post-prandial drink.

MILES
looks like he's thinking about something. Then --

                    MILES
          I hate Tony Levin.

Jack swirls his wine and downs it in one big gulp. Just
then --

MAYA walks into the bar and takes a seat a few stools
down. She has changed into a black cashmere sweater and
corduroys, lovely but tired.

                    MAYA
               (to Gary)
          Highliner, please.

                    JACK
          That's on us.

Maya looks over and smiles as Gary pours her a glass from
their bottle.

                         MAYA
              Hey, guys.

Maya gets an American Spirit Yellow out of her purse and
lights it while Gary pours her a glass.

                         MILES
              You want to join us?

                         MAYA
                    (polite)
              Sure.

In no hurry, she takes a long sip of her wine, gets up
and comes down the bar.

                         MAYA (CONT'D)
              So how's that book of yours going, Miles?
              I think you were almost done with it last
              time we talked.

                         MILES
              I finished it.

                         MAYA
              Good for you.

                         JACK
              It's getting published. That's what
              we're up here celebrating.

Miles shoots Jack a look. Jack responds with a "don't-
fuck-it-up-brother" glower.

                         MAYA
              That's fantastic. Congratulations.

She offers her glass, and all clink.

                         MAYA (CONT'D)
                    (to Jack)
              Are you a writer too?

                         JACK
              No, I'm an actor.

                         MAYA
              Oh yeah? What kind of stuff?

                         JACK
              A lot of TV. I was a regular on a couple
              of series. And lately I've been doing a
              lot of commercials. National mostly.

                              MAYA
                    Anything I'd know?

                              JACK
                    Maybe. Recognize this?

Jack takes a deep breath, and out comes a perfect VOICE-
OVER VOICE.

                         JACK (CONT'D)
                    "Now with low, low 5.8% APR financing."

Maya's mouth drops open and curves into a big smile.

                              MAYA
                    That's hilarious. You sound just like
                    one of those guys.

                              JACK
                    I am one of those guys.

                              MAYA
                    You are not.

                              MILES
                    He is.

Jack launches into another one of his sure-fire hits.

                              JACK
                         (very fast)
                    Consult your doctor before using this
                    product. Side effects may include oily
                    discharge, dizziness, hives, loss of
                    appetite, difficulty breathing and low
                    blood pressure. If you have diabetes or
                    a history of kidney trouble... you're
                    fucked!

This makes Maya laugh a big throaty laugh. Jack joins
in. Nervous about Jack's aggressive flirtatiousness,
Miles musters a tight courtesy smile.

                              MAYA
                         (winding down)
                    Oh. I needed that. Thank you.

They all take a drink of wine.

                         MAYA (CONT'D)
                    So what are you guys up to tonight?

Before Jack has a chance to speak --

                         MILES
              We're pretty wiped. Probably go back to
              the hotel and crash.

This makes Maya slightly embarrassed at her apparent
availability, but she recovers quickly, remains breezy.

                         MAYA
              Yeah, I know what you mean. It's a long
              drive up here. Where're you staying?

                         MILES
              The Windmill.

                         JACK
              Windmill.

Maya downs the rest of her wine, stamps out her smoke,
and picks up her jean jacket and purse.

                         MAYA
              Well, good to see you, Miles. Jack.

                         MILES
              See you.

As she leaves --

                         JACK
              We'll catch up with you later, okay?

But she's gone. Jack gives Miles a slow burn look.

                         JACK (CONT'D)
              We'll probably go back to the hotel and
              crash?

49   **EXT. HIGHWAY - NIGHT**   49

The guys walk drunkenly along the shoulder as CARS WHIZ BY.

                         JACK
              The girl is looking to party, and you tell
              her we're going to go back to our motel
              room and *crash*? Jesus, Miles!

                         MILES
              Well, I'm tired. Aren't you tired?

                    JACK
          The chick digs you. She lit up like a
          pinball machine when she heard your novel
          was getting published.

                    MILES
          Now I've got another lie to live down.
          Thanks, Jack.

                    JACK
          I'm trying to get you some action, but
          you've got to help me out just a little
          bit.

                    MILES
          Didn't seem to me like that's what was
          going on. You were all over her.

                    JACK
          Somebody had to do the talking. And by
          the way, I was right. She's not married.

                    MILES
          How do you know?

                    JACK
          No rock. When she came to the bar, sans rock.

INT. MOTEL ROOM -- NIGHT   50

The screen is absolutely BLACK.

                    JACK
          Single. Waitress. Getting off work. Looking
          for love. A little slap and tickle.

                    MILES
          Shut up.

                    JACK
          She probably went home, lit some candles,
          put on some relaxing music, took a nice
          hot bath, and laid down on her bed with
          her favorite vibrator.

Jack begins to make a soft BUZZING noise, growing
gradually louder and more rhythmic.

                    MILES
          Have you no shame?

                         JACK
              Oooh. Oh. Miles. Miles.

                         MILES
              Fuck you.

There's now a rustling noise and footsteps. Then a LIGHT
is flipped on in the BATHROOM.

Miles closes the door behind him, and the only light
visible is at the bottom of the bathroom door.

Miles PEES -- a series of semi-forced SHORT SQUIRTS.
Then a FLUSH as a door opens and the light goes off.
Jack starts BUZZING again.

                         MILES (CONT'D)
              Shut the fuck up!

Jack stops and Miles climbs into bed. Silence. Then --

                         JACK
              You need to get your prostate checked.

UNDER BLACK --

                         MONDAY

51   **EXT. BREAKFAST CAFE - DAY**   51

         Establishing.

52   **INT. BREAKFAST CAFE - DAY**   52

         Miles and Jack are glancing at the menus. For some
         reason Jack is humorless and grumpy.

                         MILES
                    So what're we going to have? Pigs in a
                    blanket? The "rancher's special
                    breakfast?" Or maybe just some grease
                    and fat with a side of lard?

                         JACK
                         (not amused)
                    So what's the plan today?

                         MILES
                    We head north, begin the grape tour up
                    there, make our way south so the more we
                    drink the closer we get to the motel.

Jack sarcastically taps an index finger to his temple.

                    MILES (CONT'D)
          What's your problem?

Jack exhales and looks away, as though he doesn't want to
get into it.

                    MILES (CONT'D)
          What is it?

Jack sucks his teeth a moment searching for the right
words. Then the dam bursts.

                    JACK
          I am going to get my nut on this trip,
          Miles. And you are not going to fuck it
          up for me with all your depression and
          anxiety and neg-head downer shit.

                    MILES
          Ooooh, now the cards are on the table.

                    JACK
          Yes they are. And I'm serious. Do not
          fuck with me. I am going to get laid
          before I settle down on Saturday. Do you
          read me?

                    MILES
          Sure, big guy. Whatever you say. It's your
          party. I'm sorry I'm in the way and
          dragging you down. Maybe you'd have a
          better time on your own. You take the car.
          I'll catch the train back.

                    JACK
          No, see, I want both of us to get crazy.
          We should both be cutting loose. I mean,
          this is our last chance. This is our week!
          It should be something we share.

The older WAITRESS comes over.

                    WAITRESS
          Can I take your order?

                    JACK
          But I am warning you.

                    MILES
          Oatmeal, one poached egg, and rye toast.
          Dry.

                         WAITRESS
                 Okay. And you?

                         JACK
                    (glaring at Miles)
                 Pigs in a blanket. With extra syrup.

53   **EXT. LOVELY HIGHWAY - DAY**   53

        The Saab winds along this beautiful road that meanders
        through large open vineyards.

                                          DISSOLVE TO:

54   **INSERT --**   54

        A MAP and a MOVING LINE show the boys' route.

                                          DISSOLVE TO:

55   **INSERT --**   55

        GRAPES growing on the vine.

                                          DISSOLVE TO:

56   **EXT. VINEYARD - DAY**   56

        Framed by foreground grapevines, the Saab passes in the
        distance.

                                          DISSOLVE TO:

57   **INT. FOXEN WINERY - DAY**   57

        Miles has just downed a taste of red wine.

                         MILES
                 How much skin and stem contact?

                         POURER
                 About four weeks.

                         MILES
                 Huh. That explains all the tannins. And
                 how long in oak?

                         POURER
              About a year.

                         MILES
              French or American?

                         POURER
              Both.

                         MILES
              Good stuff.

                         JACK
              Yeah, oak. That's a good wood.

Just as the pourer turns away toward other TASTERS, Jack
GRABS the bottle and helps himself and Miles to another
glass. They slam back their drinks like tequila.

                                        DISSOLVE TO:

8   **EXT. LOVELY AREA ON A HILL - DAY**   58

Miles brings the Saab to a stop, and the guys get out.
Before them lies an incredible view of endless vineyards.

                         MILES
              Nice, huh?

                         JACK
              Beautiful.

                         MILES
              Victoria and I used to like this view.
                   (lost in nostalgia)
              Once we had a picnic here and drank a '95
              Opus One. With smoked salmon and
              artichokes, but we didn't care.

                         JACK
              Miles.

                         MILES
              She has the best palate of any woman I've
              ever known. She could even differentiate
              Italian wines.

                         JACK
              Miles, I gotta tell you something.
              Victoria's coming to the wedding.

                    MILES
          I know. You told me. I'm okay with it.

                    JACK
          Yeah, but that's not the whole story. She
          got remarried.

                    MILES
          She what?
                    (long pause)
          When?

                    JACK
          About a month ago. Six weeks.

                    MILES
          To that guy? That guy with the
          restaurant...

Jack nods. Miles looks down at his shoes and draws a
long breath. Then he stiffly gets back in the open car
and closes the door.

                    JACK
          Miles... MILES...

Miles continues to stare straight ahead.

                    JACK (CONT'D)
                    (exploding)
          Jesus Christ, Miles. Get out!

                    MILES
          I want to go home now.

                    JACK
          You've been divorced for two years
          already. People move on. She has! It's
          like you enjoy self-pity. Makes you feel
          special or something.

                    MILES
          Is she bringing him to the wedding?

                    JACK
          What do you think?

                    MILES
          You drop this bombshell on me. Why
          didn't you tell me before?

                    JACK
          Because I knew you'd freak out and
          probably get so depressed you wouldn't
          even come on this trip. But then I
          figured here would be the best place to
          tell you. We're here to forget about all
          that shit. We're here to party!

                    MILES
               (undeterred)
          I'm going to be a fucking pariah.
          Everyone's just going to be holding their
          breath to see if I'm going to get drunk
          and make a scene. Plus Tony fucking
          Levin?

                    JACK
          No, no, no. It's cool. I talked to
          Victoria. She's cool. Everyone's cool.

                    MILES
               (horrified)
          You've all been *talking* about it? Behind
          my back? *Talking* about it?

Miles turns and locates an open BOTTLE of wine in the
back seat. He uncorks it and begins to swig.

                    JACK
          Hey, hey, hey. No, you don't!

Jack tries unsuccessfully to grab the bottle from Miles,
but Miles bolts out of the car.

A VERY WIDE SHOT --

Pursued by Jack, Miles dashes down the hill, all the
while taking huge swigs from the bottle.

OMIT   59

EXT. LOVELY VINEYARD -- CONTINUOUS   60

Miles slows to a walk between rows of GRAPEVINES. He
polishes off the bottle and tosses it. A panting Jack
catches up with him in the adjacent grapevine corridor.

Miles's face crumbles as though he were about to cry. Then
he collapses to the ground and closes his eyes tight.

Jack looks around impatiently for a moment. Then he squats
down so he can see Miles underneath the vines.

                              JACK
                  Miles?

Miles ignores Jack and focuses on the beautiful RIPE GRAPES
that surround him. They seem to distract him from his pain.

                          JACK (CONT'D)
                  You going to be okay?

Miles looks up and shakes his head a definitive NO. Jack
can't help but LAUGH.

                                        DISSOLVE TO:

61   **EXT. KALYRA WINERY PARKING LOT - DAY**   61

        The sun hangs low as the Saab pulls into the parking lot,
        Jack at the wheel.

62   **INT. KALYRA TASTING ROOM - DAY**   62

        The pourer, a brunette in her early thirties, breaks away
        from a BORING COUPLE down the bar. This is STEPHANIE.

                            STEPHANIE
                  Hey, guys. How's it going?

                              JACK
                  Excellent. My friend and I are up here
                  doing the wine tour, and he tells me that
                  you folks make one hell of a Syrah.

                            STEPHANIE
                  That's what people say.

                              MILES
                        (slurring slightly)
                  You gotta excuse him. Yesterday he
                  didn't know Pinot Noir from film noir.

                              JACK
                  I'm a quick learner.

        Stephanie laughs. She apparently likes big good-natured
        lunks like Jack.

                              MILES
                  I'm trying to teach my friend here some
                  basics about wine over the next few days
                  before he goes off and --

WHOOMP! Under the bar Jack stomps on Miles's foot.
Miles winces.

Stephanie slides TWO GLASSES in front of them.

                    JACK
          That's right -- I'm here to learn. I never
          had that much interest in wine before, but
          this trip has been very enlightening. Always
          liked wine, of course, but I don't know. More
          of a beer man, really. Microbreweries.

She THUMPS the cork off a bottle of Chardonnay.

                    STEPHANIE
          Well, no better way to learn than tasting.

She pours almost flirtatious amounts.

                    JACK
          Now there's a girl who knows how to pour.
          What's your name?

                    STEPHANIE
          Stephanie.

                    JACK
          Nice.

Jack swirls the wine as though he were by now a
sommelier. They look, they smell, they taste.

                    STEPHANIE
          So what do you think?

                    MILES
          Quaffable but far from transcendent.

                    JACK
          I like it. Tastes great. Oaky.

Stephanie reaches for another bottle and pours. Jack's
eyes never leave her.

                    STEPHANIE
          Cabernet Franc.
               (as they taste)
          This is only the fifth year we've made
          this varietal. Very few wineries around
          here do a straight Cabernet Franc. It's
          from our vineyard up in Santa Maria. And
          it was a Silver Medal winner at Paso
          Robles last year.

                    MILES
          Well, I've come to never expect greatness
          from a Cab Franc, and this one's no
          exception. Sort of a flabby, overripe --

                    JACK
               (ignoring him)
          Tastes good to me. You live around here, Stephanie

                    STEPHANIE
          In Santa Ynez.
               (low, to Miles)
          And I agree with you about Cab Franc.

                    JACK
          Oh yeah? We're just over in Buellton. Windmill In

                    STEPHANIE
          Oh yeah.

                    JACK
          You know a gal named Maya? Works at the
          Hitching Post?

                    STEPHANIE
          Sure I know Maya. Real well.

                    JACK
          No shit. We just had a drink with her
          last night. Miles knows her.

                    MILES
          Could we move on to the Syrah, please?

                    STEPHANIE
          Chomping at the bit, huh? Sure.

As she turns to reach for the right bottle, Jack winks at
Miles. Miles shakes his head.

                    STEPHANIE (CONT'D)
          This is our Estate Syrah...

She pours each of them a full HALF GLASS.

                    JACK
          You're a bad, bad girl, Stephanie.

                    STEPHANIE
          I know. I might need to be spanked.

She notices the boring couple, visibly annoyed that she
has been monopolized.

                    STEPHANIE (CONT'D)
          Excuse me.

As she wanders down the bar, Jack turns to Miles, his
mouth wide open.

                    JACK
          A bad girl, Miles. She might need to be
          spanked.

                    MILES
          Do you know how often these pourers get
          hit on?

They glance down the bar at Stephanie. She smiles back.

EXT. KALYRA WINERY PARKING LOT - DAY   63

Miles is killing time by the car staring at his shoes.
He looks over and sees Jack waddling over from the
tasting room with TWO CASES of wine.

                    JACK
          Get the trunk.

                    MILES
          You have the keys.

Jack puts the cases down and glances back at the building.

                    JACK
          We're on.

                    MILES
          What?

                    JACK
          She called Maya, who's not working
          tonight, so we're all going out.

                    MILES
          With Maya?

                    JACK
          Been divorced for a year now, bud.

Jack puts the wine in the trunk, and they get in the car.

                    JACK (CONT'D)
          Stephanie, holy shit. Chick has it all
          going on.

                    MILES
          Well, she is cute.

                    JACK
          Cute? She's a fucking hottie. And you
          almost tell her I'm getting married.
          What's the matter with you?
                    (drumming the steering wheel)
          Gotta love it. Gotta love it.

64   **INT. MOTEL ROOM - DAY**   64

      THE TV --
      GOLF on ESPN.

      MILES AND JACK
      sit transfixed, each on his own bed. The curtains are
      drawn. Then out of nowhere --

                    JACK
                    (mocking)
          You know how often these pourers get hit
          on?
                    (getting up)
          I'm going for a swim. Get the blood
          flowing. Want to come?

                    MILES
          Nah. I want to watch this.

      CLOSE ON THE TV --
      A guy gets ready to putt. The announcer whispers what an
      important moment this is. The guy misses.

                                        FADE TO BLACK.

65   **UNDER BLACK --**   65

      The sound of an AEROSOL CAN.

                    JACK
          Miles. Hey, Miles. Time to get up.

      WE OPEN OUR EYES TO SEE --
      Jack spraying his feet with some Dr. Scholl's product.

      WIDE --

      Miles pulls himself out of bed and slouches toward his
      suitcase.

                              JACK (CONT'D)
          Fucking chick in the Jacuzzi -- goddamn,
          Miles, fucking going nuts up here. Whole
          place is wide open. Assylvania.

Jack does some actor's weird warm-up stretch.

                              MILES
          So what should I wear?

                              JACK
          I don't know. Casual but nice. They
          think you're a writer.

As Miles begins to dig through his suitcase, Jack flips
open his cellphone and speed-dials.

                              JACK (CONT'D)
          Don't you have any other shoes?

Miles glances at his shoes sitting sadly on the floor.

                              JACK (CONT'D)
                    (into the phone)
          Hello? Oh hey, baby, just checking in.
          Not much. We're about to go out for
          dinner, probably be out pretty late, so
          I thought I'd say goodnight now. I
          know, I love you too. I miss you.

EXT. LOS OLIVOS - NIGHT   66

The boys get out of the car and walk along a timbered
sidewalk in this tourist town with wine tasting rooms and
gourmet restaurants.

                              JACK
          Please just try to be your normal humorous
          self, okay? Like who you were before the
          tailspin. Do you remember that guy?
          People love that guy. And don't forget --
          your novel is coming out in the fall.

                              MILES
          Oh yeah? How exciting. What's it
          called?

                              JACK
          Do not sabotage me. If you want to be a
          lightweight, that's your call. But do
          not sabotage me.

                        MILES
          Aye-aye, captain.

                        JACK
          And if they want to drink Merlot, we're
          drinking Merlot.

                        MILES
                    (dead serious)
          If anyone orders Merlot, I'm leaving. I
          am not drinking any fucking Merlot!

                        JACK
          Okay, okay. Relax, Miles, Jesus. No
          Merlot. Did you bring your Xanax?

Miles takes a SMALL BOTTLE from his pocket and rattles it.

                        JACK (CONT'D)
          And don't drink too much. I don't want you
          going to the dark side or passing out. Do
          you hear me? No going to the dark side.

                        MILES
          Okay! Fuck!

Miles quickly POPS A XANAX. Jack gives him a final look
in the eye.

                        JACK
          We're going in.

67   **INT. LOS OLIVOS CAFE - NIGHT**   67

The boys enter this cozy if crowded restaurant and
exchange words with the HOSTESS. Then they notice --

MAYA AND STEPHANIE
at a booth waving at them. They look great.

MILES AND JACK
make their way to the table, Jack wearing a broad,
confident SMILE.

AT THE TABLE --

Jack plops down next to Stephanie, while Miles politely
eases in on Maya's side. Jack touches a hand to
Stephanie's bare neck and massages it meaningfully.

                        JACK
          How you doin' tonight, beautiful?

                         STEPHANIE
          Good. How're you?

                         JACK
          Great. You look great.
                    (including Maya)
          You both do.

                         STEPHANIE
          Not so bad yourself.

Meanwhile Miles looks over at Maya and purses his lips in
an affable if uncomfortable smile. Then --

                         MILES
          What are you drinking?

                         MAYA
          A Fiddlehead Sauvignon Blanc.

                         MILES
          Oh yeah? How is it?

                         MAYA
                    (sliding the glass)
          Try it.

As Miles swirls the wine and takes a sip, he begins to
relax.

                         MILES
          Nice. Very nice.

                         MAYA
          Twelve months in oak.

                         MILES
          On a Sauvignon Blanc?

                         MAYA
          I know the winemaker. She comes in the
          restaurant all the time.

                         MILES
          This is good. Little hints of clove.

                         MAYA
          I know. I love that.

LATER --

A WAITER finishes listing off the specials.

                              WAITER
          ... medallions of pork with a dusting of
          black truffles served with a root
          vegetable *foulon* and wasabi-whipped
          potatoes. And finally a Copper River
          salmon grilled on an alder wood plank.
          And that comes with roasted new potatoes
          and steamed watercress.

The four diners exchange looks of delight.

                         WAITER (CONT'D)
          And who gets the wine list?

Miles raises his hand and takes the leather-bound book.

                              MAYA
                         (teasing)
          I guess Miles wants it.

Jack glares at Miles, who immediately gets the hint.

                              MILES
          Nope. You ladies choose.

Jack smiles and nods his approval. Jack takes the book
out of Miles's hands and offers it to the girls.

                              MAYA
          You choose, Stephanie.

                            STEPHANIE
                         (opening it)
          So what does everyone feel like?

                              JACK
          Whatever you girls want. It's on us
          tonight. Sky's the limit.

                              MAYA
          No, we're paying for the wine.

                              JACK
          I don't think so. We're celebrating Miles's
          book deal.

                              MAYA
          Well, in that case...

Miles draws a long breath.

                              STEPHANIE
                    What's everyone ordering?   Then we can
                    sort out the wine.

                              MILES
                    Exactement!

Jack shoots Miles a look.

                              MAYA
                    I'm having the salmon.

                              MILES
                    That's what I'm having.

                              STEPHANIE
                         (still scanning the wines)
                    I'm thinking about the duck breast.

                              JACK
                         (slapping his menu shut)
                    Me too.

                              STEPHANIE
                    Well, that narrows things down.

Stephanie lowers the menu so that only her eyes peer over
the top. She looks at the others, and they look back at
her.

                         STEPHANIE (CONT'D)
                    Sounds like... Pinot Noir to me.

Jack looks at Miles and raises one hand for a HIGH-FIVE.

                              JACK
                    Pinot!

Miles reluctantly slaps Jack's hand. This causes the
girls to laugh. MUSIC STARTS -- they're OFF!

DINNER is improvised, but includes:

-- The arrival of the FIRST WINE.

-- The SALADS.

-- Maya takes a turn with the wine list. Miles pushes
her finger down into the prices with THREE DIGITS.

-- New stemware is provided with the arrival of the
SECOND WINE.

-- The four of them DRINK. Particularly Miles.

-- Stephanie and Jack get cozier and cozier.

-- The SALMON and DUCK arrive.

-- Miles is too shy to look into Maya's eyes. She's interested and available -- it's too much for him.

-- As Miles gets DRUNKER, the camera angles become sloppier, the cutting choppier.

-- Miles PONTIFICATES about some aspect of wine that Maya and Stephanie find interesting. Left out in the cold, his jaw tight, Jack wants to find a way in but can't.

-- Miles reaches over to refill his glass, but Jack's arm shoots out to stop him -- "Slow down."

CLOSE ON MILES as a distant RUMBLE begins to sound, the rumble of an oncoming ANXIETY ATTACK. By now he has drunk so much that he spaces out, descending into --

68   **INT. UNDERWORLD -- DARK AND TIMELESS**   68

Miles is boarding an OPEN BOAT atop this underground river, the River Styx. Just beyond a ghoulish HUMAN CARGO the hooded boatman CHARON wields a long staff. Miles is crossing over to the dark side.

69   **INT. LOS OLIVOS CAFE - BACK AGAIN**   69

Miles returns to earth to find Jack and Stephanie now in their own little world -- Jack explaining something to Stephanie that she finds fascinating, just FASCINATING.

-- Miles converses with Maya, but it's clear from her bemused expression that he's being charming if not entirely coherent.

-- ANOTHER WINE reaches the table -- a Comte Armand Pommard.

-- Miles looks over at Jack and Stephanie. They share a short but sensual kiss.

MOMENTS LATER --

Miles is on his feet threading his way through the tables. He is very unsteady, and we cut between first and third person perspectives.

AT THE BATHROOMS --

He tries the MEN'S ROOM door but it's locked. He pulls the
XANAX out of his pocket and pops one in his mouth, swallowing
it dry.

He notices a PAYPHONE nearby. Thinking better of it for a
moment, Miles makes a drunken bee-line for the receiver.

CLOSE ON THE KEYPAD --
as many numbers are dialed, and we HEAR the TONES,
completely out of sync, along with a sound melange of
interior phone RINGING and a PICKUP.

THE RECEIVER --
as Miles presses it desperately to his head.

                    VICTORIA (ON THE PHONE)
          Hello?

                    MILES
          Victoria.

                    VICTORIA (ON THE PHONE)
          Miles?

Miles feigns an implausible upbeat tone.

                    MILES
          Victoria! How the hell are you?

                    VICTORIA (ON THE PHONE)
          Fine. What's, uh, what's on your mind?

                    MILES
          Heard you got remarried! Congratulations.
          Didn't think you had the stomach for
          another go-round.

                    VICTORIA (ON THE PHONE)
          Oh, Miles. You're drunk.

                    MILES
          Just some local Pinot, you know, then a
          little Burgundy. That old Cotes de
          Beaune!

Miles laughs at his own non-existent joke.

                    VICTORIA (ON THE PHONE)
          Where are you?

                    MILES
A little place in Los Olivos. New
owners. Cozy ambiance. Excellent food
too -- you should try it. Thought of you
at the Hitching Post last night.

Silence.

                    MILES (CONT'D)
Hello?

                    VICTORIA (ON THE PHONE)
Miles, don't call me when you're drunk.

                    MILES
I just wanted you to know I've decided
not to go to the wedding, so in case you
were dreading some uncomfortable, you
know, run-in or something, well, worry no
more. You won't see me there. My
wedding gift to you and what's-his-name.
What is his name?

                    VICTORIA (ON THE PHONE)
        (silence, then --)
Ken.

                    MILES
Ken.

                    VICTORIA (ON THE PHONE)
Miles, I don't care if you come to the
wedding or not.

                    MILES
Well, I'm not coming, Barbie. So you guys
have fun.

                    VICTORIA (ON THE PHONE)
I'm going to hang up now, Miles.

                    MILES
        (rushing to keep her on)
You see, Vicki, I just heard about this
today, you getting married that is, and I
was kind of taken aback. Kind of hard to
believe.

Silence.

                         MILES (CONT'D)
          I guess I just thought there was still
          some hope for us somewhere down the road
          and I just, I just --

                         VICTORIA (ON THE PHONE)
          Miles, maybe it is better if you don't
          come to the wedding.

Miles sucks something from between his two front teeth.

                         MILES
          Whatever you say, Vicki. You're the boss.

He HANGS UP as nonchalantly as if it had been a sales
call and heads back to the table.

EXT. DEEP CANYON - DAY   70

For a flash, Miles is walking an unstable, narrow ROPE
BRIDGE extending vertiginously across a great CHASM.

INT. LOS OLIVOS CAFE - BACK AGAIN   71

Miles reaches the table, tries to sit and SLIPS ONTO THE
FLOOR. Although at first Jack blinks heavily in disgust,
the girls burst into hysterical LAUGHTER. Jack then
laughs too, perhaps OVER-LAUGHING.

                         JACK
          Easy, boy. Easy.

Maya helps him back into the booth.

                         MAYA
          Are you all right?

                         MILES
          Fine. Just slipped.
               (picking up his glass)
          This is my blood.

Miles drinks. Stephanie makes a head gesture to Maya,
who nods in return.

                         STEPHANIE
               (to the guys)
          Excuse us.

                         MAYA
          Sorry to make you get up again, Miles.

                         MILES
              That's okay.

Miles and Jack allow the girls to pass. Then --

                         JACK
              What the fuck, man? What is up?

Miles reaches for his wine glass, but Jack moves it away.

                         JACK (CONT'D)
              Pull yourself together, man.

                         MILES
              I'm fine!

But in throwing open his arms for emphasis, he spills a
WATER GLASS. Jack rights it and throws a napkin on the
tablecloth.

                         JACK
              Where were you?

                         MILES
              Bathroom.

                         JACK
              Did you drink and dial?

Miles's silence confirms his guilt and shame.

                         JACK (CONT'D)
              Why do you always do this? Victoria's
              gone, man. Gone. Poof.

Miles looks down and squeezes his eyes tight while
pushing out an exhale through his nose.

                         JACK (CONT'D)
              Stop it. You are blowing a great
              opportunity here, Miles. Fucking Maya,
              man. She's great. She's cool. She's
              funny. She knows wine. What is this
              morose come-down bullshit? These girls
              want to party. And what was that fucking
              ten-minute lecture on, what was it,
              Vouvrays? I mean, come on!

                         MILES
              Let's just say I'm uncomfortable with the
              whole scenario.

                    JACK
          Oh Jesus, Miles.

Miles belligerently reaches for his Comte Armand. Jack
lets it pass.

                    JACK (CONT'D)
          And don't forget all the bad times you
          had with Victoria. How small she made
          you feel. That's why you had the affair
          in the first place.

                    MILES
          Shut up. Shut your face.

                    JACK
          Don't you see how Maya's looking at you?
          You got her on the hook. Reel her in!
          Come on, let's ratchet this up a notch.
          You know how to do it. Here.
                    (passing a glass)
          Drink some agua.

Miles looks at the water, takes it and drains it.

The girls now return to the table. The guys slide over.

                    MILES
                    (trying to appear sober)
          Should we get dessert?

                    STEPHANIE
          We were thinking. Why don't we go back
          to my place? I've got wine, some insane
          cheeses, music, whatever.

Jack raises both arms like a football referee.

                    JACK
          Excellent idea. Waiter!

INT. SAAB - NIGHT   72

THROUGH THE WINDSHIELD --

Trees and bushes lit by the headlights show us we're
headed into the woods.

INSIDE --

Jack drives. Miles blinks heavily as he tries to make
sense of A HAND-DRAWN MAP.

                         JACK
                  (grabbing the map)
            Let me see that.

73   **EXT. STEPHANIE'S HOUSE - NIGHT**   73

      The Saab pulls into a gravel DRIVEWAY and comes to a stop
      outside this wood-framed cottage.

      Jack and Miles get out and head for the front door. On
      the way, Jack reaches into his coat pocket and produces a
      string of FOUR CONDOMS.

                         JACK
                    (tearing)
            Here. One for you, three for me.

      Miles wordlessly takes his. Just before they climb the
      porch steps --

                         MILES
            You sure you want to do this?

      Jack stops and looks at him for a moment with almost
      hostile incredulity.

      THE FRONT DOOR is open. Jack knocks twice on the SCREEN
      DOOR before going in.

74   **INT. STEPHANIE'S LIVING ROOM - CONTINUOUS**   74

      The boys enter this modest living room furnished with
      weathered but charming old furniture. Scattered here and
      there are CHILDREN'S TOYS. FINGER-PAINTINGS are taped to
      the walls. CANDLES are lit, and MUSIC is playing.

                         JACK
            We're here!

      Stephanie sails in.

                         STEPHANIE
            What happened to you guys?

                         JACK
            Couple of wrong turns.
                    (pointing a thumb at Miles)
            Thanks to Magellan, here.

      After a brief hug, Stephanie and Jack peck-kiss.

                    JACK (CONT'D)
          Hi.

                    STEPHANIE
          Hi.
                (to Miles)
          Maya's in the kitchen.

Miles hesitates a moment before Jack elbows him toward --

INT. STEPHANIE'S KITCHEN - CONTINUOUS   75

Miles wanders in to find Maya squatting in front of a
little temperature-controlled WINE STORAGE UNIT.

                    MILES
          Hi.

                    MAYA
          Hey.

                    MILES
          She got anything good?

                    MAYA
          Oh, yeah. Steph's way into Pinots and
          Syrahs.
                (calling out)
          Hey, Steph? You sure we can open
          anything? Anything we want?

                    STEPHANIE (V.O.)
          Anything but the Jayer Richebourg!

                    MILES
          She has a Richebourg? Mon dieu. I
          have completely underestimated
          Stephanie.

                    MAYA
          Who do you think you're dealing with
          here?

Maya slips out a bottle of ESCHEVAUX.

                    MAYA (CONT'D)
          How about this?

Miles nods vigorously. Maya looks back and forth
between Miles and the wine, her eyes narrowed. Then she
slides it back in.

                         MAYA (CONT'D)
          Nope. I don't think we know each other
          well enough.
                    (picking out another bottle)
          I'd say this guy's more our speed.

They rise, and Miles glances at the ANDREW MURRAY SYRAH and,
raising his eyebrows, agrees. Maya begins opening it.

                         MAYA (CONT'D)
          So what gems do you have in your collection?

                         MILES
          Not much of a collection really. I
          haven't had the wallet for that, so I
          sort of live bottle to bottle. But I've
          got a couple things I'm saving. I guess
          the star would be a 1961 Cheval Blanc.

                         MAYA
          You've got a '61 Cheval Blanc that's just
          sitting there? Go get it.
                    (pushing him, playfully stern)
          Right now. Hurry up...

Miles laughs, fights back a bit.

                         MAYA (CONT'D)
          Seriously, the '61s are peaking, aren't
          they? At least that's what I've read.

                         MILES
          Yeah, I know.

                         MAYA
          It might be too late already. What are
          you waiting for?

                         MILES
          I don't know. Special occasion. With
          the right person. It was supposed to be
          for my tenth wedding anniversary.

Understanding, Maya considers her response.

                         MAYA
          The day you open a '61 Cheval Blanc,
          that's the special occasion.

                         MILES
          How long have you been into wine?

                    MAYA
          I started to get serious about seven
          years ago.

                    MILES
          What was the bottle that did it?

                    MAYA
          Eighty-eight Sassicaia.

Miles whistles and raises his eyebrows. Maya pours, and
they clink their glasses together before savoring the
wine.

                    MILES
          Wow. We gotta give it a moment, but this
          is tasty. Really good. How about you?

                    MAYA
                (tastes again)
          I think they overdid it a bit. Too much
          alcohol. Overwhelms the fruit.

                    MILES
                (tasting again, impressed)
          Yeah, I'd say you're right on the money.

Then Miles absently scans the REFRIGERATOR DOOR and spots
a PHOTO of Stephanie holding a LITTLE GIRL.

                    MILES (CONT'D)
          Is this Stephanie's kid? Sure is cute.

                    MAYA
          Yeah, Siena's a sweetie.

                    MILES
          Is she sleeping or...?

                    MAYA
          She's with her grandmother. She's with
          Steph's mom. She spends a lot of time over
          there. Steph's... well, she's Stephanie.

Jack's voice-over voice from the other room...

                    JACK (O.S.)
          "And now for a low, low 4.8% APR..."

... is followed by PEALS OF LAUGHTER.

                    MAYA
          You got kids?

                              MILES
                    Who me? Nah, I'd just fuck them up.
                    That was the one unpolluted part of my
                    divorce -- no kids.

                              MAYA
                    Yeah, same here.

Maya nods as she sips again, looking distant for a
moment, thinking about something else.

                              MAYA (CONT'D)
                    Let's go in there.

Maya takes the bottle, and they wander into --

76   **INT. STEPHANIE'S LIVING ROOM - CONTINUOUS**   76

Jack and Maya are gone. From a distant bedroom comes
more laughter.

                              MAYA
                    Looks like our friends are hitting it
                    off.

While Maya goes to turn down the STEREO, Miles sits on the
couch. Maya's shirt rides up as she crouches, giving Miles
a glimpse of the SMALL OF HER BACK.

She takes a seat opposite Miles on the couch. They look at
each other without speaking. Just what *is* the vibe here?

                              MAYA (CONT'D)
                    It's kind of weird sitting here with you
                    in Stephanie's house. All those times
                    you came into the restaurant. It's like
                    you're a real person now. Almost.

                              MILES
                    Yeah, I know. It's kind of weird. Out
                    of context.

                              MAYA
                    Yeah, weird. But great.

                              MILES
                    Yeah. Definitely.

An awkward silence, broken by Maya.

                              MAYA
                    So what's your novel about?

                    MILES
Well, it's a little difficult to
summarize. It begins as a first-person
account of a guy taking care of his
father after a stroke. Kind of based on
personal experience, but only loosely.

                    MAYA
What's the title?

                    MILES
"The Day After Yesterday."

                    MAYA
Oh. You mean... today?

                    MILES
Um... yeah but it's more...

                    MAYA
So is it kind of about death and
mortality, or...?

                    MILES
Mmmm, yeah... but not really. It shifts
around a lot. Like you also start to see
everything from the point of view of the
father. And some other stuff happens,
some parallel narrative, and then it
evolves -- or devolves -- into a kind of
a Robbe-Grillet mystery -- you know, with
no real resolution.

                    MAYA
Wow. Anyway, I think it's amazing you're
getting it published. Really. I know
how hard it is. Just to write it even.

                    MILES
          (squeezing it out)
Yeah. Thanks.

                    MAYA
Like me, I have this stupid paper due on
Friday, and as usual I'm freaked out
about it. Just like in high school. It
never changes.

                    MILES
A paper?

                    MAYA
          Yeah. I'm working on a masters in
          Horticulture. Chipping away at it.

                    MILES
          Horticulture? Wow. I didn't know there
          was a college here.

                    MAYA
          I commute to San Luis Obispo twice a
          week.

                    MILES
          So... you want to work for a winery or
          something someday?

                    MAYA
                (smiling, coy)
          Maybe. So when can I read your book?

                    MILES
          Well... I do have a copy of the
          manuscript in the car. It's not fully
          proofed, but if you're okay with a few
          typos...

                    MAYA
          Oh yeah. Who cares? I'm the queen of
          typos.
                (sipping the wine)
          Wow, this is really starting to open up.
          What do you think?

                    MILES
          My palate's kind of shot, but from what I
          can tell, I'd dub it pretty damn good.

                    MAYA
          Can I ask you a personal question?

                    MILES
                (bracing himself)
          Sure.

                    MAYA
          Why are you so into Pinot? It's like a
          thing with you.

Miles laughs at first, then smiles wistfully at the
question. He searches for the answer in his glass and
begins slowly.

STILLS

Paul Giamatti as Miles and Thomas Haden Church as Jack.

Sandra Oh as Stephanie.

Virginia Madsen as Maya.

Giamatti, Church, and Alexander Payne rehearse at Sanford.

Madsen in uniform at The Hitching Post.

Payne and Giamatti at The Hitching Post.

Payne, Cinematographer Phedon Papamichael, Giamatti, and Church plan a shot.

Church and Giamatti at Kalyra's tasting room.

Church and Giamatti run for the hills.

Giamatti and Church contemplate Miles's misfortune at the beach.

Giamatti and Church discuss Jack's reservations about his impending wedding.

Giamatti and Church take a break at Alisal golf course in Solvang.

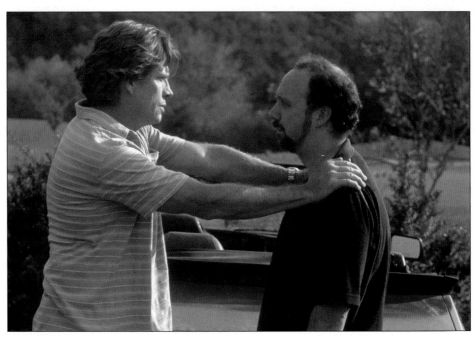

Church and Giamatti back in character.

Payne, Papamichael, and Co-Producer/First Assistant Director George Parra.

Giamatti and Madsen at the Los Olivos Cafe.

Oh and Church at the Los Olivos Cafe.

Payne rehearses with the actors at a scenic location in the Valley.

The Sideways crew captures the setting sun.

Church and Oh train for a scene.

Madsen, Giamatti, Church, and Oh at Firestone Winery.

Exploring Firestone's barrel room.

Payne preparing a shot near wine tanks.

Oh, Church, Giamatti, and Madsen at Stephanie's house.

Giamatti and Madsen in a walnut orchard...

...and at a farmer's market in Lompoc.

Giamatti and actor Joe Marinelli rehearse at Fess Parker Winery ("Frass Canyon").

Giamatti gets cleaned up after drinking the spit bucket.

Payne rehearses with actor MC Gainey at a location in Lompoc.

Giamatti and Church at A. J. Spur's in Buellton.

Alysia Reiner (as Christine) and Church.

Paul Giamatti as Miles Raymond.

Giamatti, Payne, and Church at Foxen Winery.

Giamatti, Payne, and Church.

Key Grip Ray Garcia, Factotum Tracy Boyd, Director of Photography Phedon Papamichael, Chief Lighting Technician Rafael Sanchez, Director Alexander Payne, and Co-Producer/First Assistant Director George Parra.

Church and Giamatti rehearse a scene cut from the film.

Giamatti, Madsen, Payne, Church's hair, and Oh at Firestone.

Payne and Parra.

Sideways novelist Rex Pickett with Payne and Producer Michael London.

Alexander Payne among the grapes.

                    MILES
          I don't know. It's a hard grape to grow. As
          you know. It's thin-skinned, temperamental,
          ripens early. It's not a survivor like
          Cabernet that can grow anywhere and thrive
          even when neglected. Pinot needs constant
          care and attention and in fact can only grow
          in specific little tucked-away corners of the
          world. And only the most patient and   *
          nurturing growers can do it really, can tap   *
          into Pinot's most fragile, delicate qualities.   *
          Only when someone has taken the time to truly   *
          understand its potential can Pinot be coaxed   *
          into its fullest expression. And when that   *
          happens, its flavors are the most haunting and   *
          brilliant and subtle and thrilling and ancient
          on the planet.

Maya has found this answer revealing and moving.

                    MILES (CONT'D)
          I mean, Cabernets can be powerful and
          exalting, but they seem prosaic to me for
          some reason. By comparison. How about
          you?

                    MAYA
          What about me?

                    MILES
          I don't know. Why are you into wine?

                    MAYA
          I suppose I got really into wine
          originally through my ex-husband. He had
          a big, kind of show-off cellar. But then
          I found out that I have a really sharp
          palate, and the more I drank, the more I
          liked what it made me think about.

                    MILES
          Yeah? Like what?

                    MAYA
          Like what a fraud he was.   *

Miles laughs.   *

                    MAYA   *
          No, but I do like to think about the life   *
          of wine, how it's a living thing.   *
                    (MORE)

                              MAYA (CONT'D)
          I like to think about what was going on
          the year the grapes were growing, how the
          sun was shining that summer or if it
          rained... what the weather was like. I
          think about all those people who tended
          and picked the grapes, and if it's an old
          wine, how many of them must be dead by
          now. I love how wine continues to evolve,
          how every time I open a bottle it's going
          to taste different than if I had opened it
          on any other day. Because a bottle of
          wine is actually alive -- it's constantly
          evolving and gaining complexity. That
          is, until it peaks -- like your '61 -- and
          begins its steady, inevitable decline.
          And it tastes so fucking good.

Now it is Miles's turn to be swept away. Maya's face
tells us the moment is right, but Miles remains frozen.
He needs another sign, and Maya is bold enough to offer
it: she reaches out and places one hand atop his.

                              MILES
                      (suppressing his panic)
          But I like a lot of wines besides Pinot too.
          Lately I've really been into Rieslings. Do
          you like Rieslings? Rieslings?

She nods, a Mona Lisa smile on her lips. Come on, Miles.
Finally --

                              MILES (CONT'D)
                      (pointing)
          Bathroom over there?

                              MAYA
          Yeah.

Miles gets up and walks out. Maya sighs and gets an
American Spirit out of her purse.

77   **INT. STEPHANIE'S BATHROOM - NIGHT**   77

The bathroom's a MESS -- the shower curtain is filthy,
and the chipped and water-stained tub is filled with
CHILDREN'S BATH TOYS.

Miles is bent over the sink splashing water on his face,
trying to sober up and gather his courage. He stands, and
without drying his face, presses his palms against his
cheeks. Then he takes a deep breath and drops his hands.

> MILES
> You are such a loser. Come on!

INT. THE LIVING ROOM - NIGHT   78

Miles comes out of the bathroom and looks for Maya, but
she's not there.

Then he hears a noise from the kitchen, so he goes
through the door into --

INT. STEPHANIE'S KITCHEN - CONTINUOUS   79

Maya is at the sink, filling a glass with water.

> MAYA
> I was just getting some water.
> You want some water?

Miles goes to stand by her and accepts a glass of water.
Just as she's about to fill a second glass, he stops her
and looks her in the eye, trying to recapture a moment
that is long gone.

He kisses her and she kisses back, but the whole thing
feels strained and awkward.

After a few seconds, Maya breaks away.

> MAYA (CONT'D)
> Nice.

But instead of resuming the kiss, she steps past him,
heading back into the living room.

> MAYA (O.S.) (CONT'D)
> I should probably get going.

Miles realizes he's blown it and silently berates
himself.

INT. SAAB - NIGHT   80

Miles drives down the hill behind Maya's car, which leads
him through this very rural road.

81   **EXT. WHERE THE ROAD MEETS THE HIGHWAY -- NIGHT**   81

Maya's car comes to a stop just ahead of the Saab. She
puts it in PARK and gets out.

AT THE SAAB --

Miles rolls down his window as Maya leans over.

                    MAYA
          You know how to get back to the Windmill,
          right?
                    (pointing)
          Two rights and a left.

                    MILES
          Got it.

                    MAYA
          I had a good time tonight, Miles. I
          really did.

                    MILES
          Good. So did I.

                    MAYA
          Okay. See you around.

                    MILES
          Um... did you still want to read my
          novel?

                    MAYA
          Oh, yeah. Sure. Of course.

Miles turns to the backseat, locates a large MANUSCRIPT
BOX, and hands it to Maya.

                    MAYA (CONT'D)
          Wow. Great.

                    MILES
          Just a second.

He turns around again, produces a SECOND BOX, and hands
it over as well.

                    MILES (CONT'D)
          Hope you like it. Feel free to stop
          reading at any time. I'll take no
          offense.

                    MAYA
          Goodnight, Miles.

She gives him a friendly peck on the cheek.

After she gets back in her car, she heads in one
direction while Miles heads in the opposite.

OMIT   82

UNDER BLACK --

                    TUESDAY

Jack's cellphone RINGS.

INT. MOTEL ROOM - MORNING   83

NOW EARLY MORNING --

Still fully clothed, Miles staggers across the room.

Fishing the phone out of Jack's windbreaker pocket, he
looks at the CALLER ID: "Erganian, Christine" and the
number. He briefly considers his options -- answer it?
shut it off? -- before placing it atop Jack's suitcase.

The moment he lies back down on the bed, the MOTEL PHONE
RINGS. An old DIGITAL CLOCK next to it reads 7:10.

As Miles closes his eyes and pulls the pillow over his
aching head, we again --

                              FADE TO BLACK.

LATER --   83A

VROOM!
Outside a roaring MOTORCYCLE comes to a stop. Then over
the sound of an IDLING ENGINE come familiar if indistinct
VOICES and LAUGHTER.

Miles opens his bleary eyes and listens.

FOOTSTEPS pound on the balcony outside, and Jack lets
himself in, flushed and exuberant.

                    JACK
          Fucking chick is unbelievable. Un-be-
          lieve-able!

He pounds the wall, then goes into the bathroom and
without closing the door unzips his pants to PEE.

                         JACK (CONT'D)
              Goddamn, Miles, she is nasty. Nasty
              nasty nasty.

                         MILES
              Well, I'm glad you got it out of your system.
              Congratulations. Mission accomplished.

A hungover Miles gets up and looks out the door Jack has
left open. Down in the parking lot he sees --

STEPHANIE
atop a mid-sized MOTORCYCLE, wearing a weathered fringed
suede jacket. She gives him a big friendly WAVE.

MILES
returns the wave and goes back inside.

                         MILES (CONT'D)
              You didn't invite Stephanie to come with
              us, did you?

With a FLUSH Jack emerges from the bathroom and opens his bag

                         JACK
              Oh, hey, change of plans. Steph's off
              today, so she and I are going on a hike.

                         MILES
              We were supposed to play golf.

                         JACK
              You go. In fact, use my clubs. They're
              brand new -- gift from Christine's dad.
                    (slapping some cash on the
                     dresser)
              It's on me. Oh, say, by the way,
              Stephanie and me were thinking we'd all
              go to the Hitching Post tonight and sit
              at one of Maya's tables, and she'll bring
              us some great wines and then we can all --

                         MILES
                    (sitting down)
              Count me out.

                         JACK
              Oooh, I see. Didn't go so good last night,
              huh? That's a shocker.
                    (MORE)

                          JACK (CONT'D)
          You mean getting drunk and calling Victoria
          didn't put you in the mood? You dumb fuck.
          Your divorce pain's getting real old real
          fast, dude.

Miles looks down. Jack heads for the door.

                          JACK (CONT'D)
          Later.

                          MILES
          Yeah, well, maybe you should check your
          messages first.

Jack stops, eyeing Miles suspiciously. Miles tosses Jack
his phone. Jack flips it open and scrolls down with his
thumb. He doesn't like what he sees.

                          JACK
          Oh, boy.

                          MILES
               (pointing at the room phone)
          She's been leaving messages here too.

                          JACK
          Yeah. Okay.

He SNAPS the phone shut and puts it back.

                          MILES
          You should call her.

                          JACK
          I will.
               (heading out the door)
          See ya!

                          MILES
          Right now.

                          JACK
          Okay! Jesus!

Jack picks up his phone, sits on the bed and looks
defiantly at Miles.

                          JACK (CONT'D)
          I've got no problem calling her.

Now Jack closes his eyes and brings the heel of his hand
to his forehead as he begins to concoct the BIG LIE.

                              JACK (CONT'D)
                          (opening his phone)
                    Wait outside, will you?

84   **EXT. WINDMILL INN - DAY**   84

Miles wanders out and looks down at Stephanie.

                              STEPHANIE
                    That was fun last night.

                              MILES
                    Yeah. Good food. You've got quite a
                    wine collection. Very impressive.

                              STEPHANIE
                    Thanks. Hey, I talked to Maya this
                    morning. She said she had a good time
                    too. You should call her.

Miles says nothing.

                              STEPHANIE (CONT'D)
                    Where's Jack?

                              MILES
                    Had to make a phone call.

Stephanie cuts her bike's engine and climbs off, propping
it up on the kickstand.

                              STEPHANIE
                    So what are you up to today, Miles?

                              MILES
                    Just kickin' back, I guess. I don't
                    know. Jack and I were supposed to go
                    golfing.

                              STEPHANIE
                    Huh.

                              MILES
                    Yeah, I reserved the tee time about a
                    month ago.

                              STEPHANIE
                    Oops. Sorry.

                              MILES
                    You golf?

>   STEPHANIE
> Me? No, I think it's kind of a stupid
> game. I mean, at least, I could never
> get into it. I tried it once.

>   MILES
> Huh. Jack loves golf. Crazy about it.

Just then Jack cracks open the motel room door.

>   JACK
>   (hushed)
> Hey Miles. Miles.

Miles ducks back inside.

INT. MOTEL ROOM - CONTINUOUS   85

>   JACK
> Do you have that other condom?

Miles reaches into his wallet and hands over the little
foil square.

>   MILES
> What'd Christine say?

>   JACK
> Lucked out -- got voice mail.
> Everything's cool.

EXT. WINDMILL INN - CONTINUOUS   86

Jack bounds out of the room and down the stairs like a
child on Christmas morning.

Miles watches Jack climb on the bike behind Stephanie,
grasping her waist. Stephanie kicks the starter and revs
the engine like a pro.

Stephanie and Jack PEEL OUT, leaving Miles alone on the
balcony.

CLOSE ON MILES --

As we begin to hear a SNIPPING sound which carries us to --

87   **EXT. MOTEL ROOM BALCONY - DAY**   87

Miles sits outside carefully trimming his toenails.
SNIP, SNIP, SNIP.   MUSIC BEGINS for this mournful
montage of solitude.

88   **INT. MOTEL LOBBY - DAY**   88

Miles takes a styrofoam cup and helps himself to a cup of
complimentary COFFEE from a PUMP THERMOS.

Then he takes a look at the rack of pamphlets of local
TOURIST ATTRACTIONS -- a water park, a mystery cave, and
of course winery after winery.

89   **EXT. WINDMILL INN JACUZZI - DAY**   89

Amid turbulent water, Miles corrects his students'
papers. He is alone in the tub, but at the nearby pool
STOCKY KIDS play noisily with SUPER-SOAKERS.

OVER MILES'S SHOULDER --

The PAPER he's reading is marked up with circled spelling
errors, and one entire paragraph has been crossed out.
Finding a new error, Miles writes "NO!!!"

CAMERA PANS to reveal a STACK of papers already heavily
marked with corrections, some of them mottled with water
stains.

90   **INT. MOTEL ROOM - DAY**   90

Miles FLOSSES, his lips pulled back into a grotesque
moue. Then he brushes with a SONIC-CARE TOOTHBRUSH.

LATER --

Miles checks his machine.

                              SYNTHESIZED VOICE (O.S.)
                    No new messages.

He hangs up, disgusted.

91   **EXT. CHINA PANDA RESTAURANT - DAY**   91

A small Buellton eatery.

INT. CHINA PANDA - DAY   92

The only customer right now, Miles eats awkwardly with
his chopsticks.

EXT. DRIVING RANGE - DAY   93

Miles DRIVES ball after ball, unsuccessfully trying to
release his frustration.

EXT. BUCOLIC ROAD - DAY   94

The Saab roars past us, perhaps going a little too fast.

INT. SAAB - CONTINUOUS   95

Whistling absently as he drives, Miles leans over to turn
the radio on and fiddle around to find a good station.
Then all of a sudden --

WHUMP! The car has struck something with a hideous sound
followed immediately by the receding "ARF-ARF-ARF-ARF" of
an injured DOG in the Saab's wake. Miles applies the
BRAKES.

EXT. BUCOLIC ROAD - DAY   96

Miles gets out of his car just in time to see --

A DOG
scampering into the nearby woods.

Miles looks around -- has anyone seen him? Is there a
nearby residence? Finding nothing, Miles momentarily
weighs his options before finally GIVING CHASE.

He follows the path of the dog into --

EXT. ROADSIDE WOODS - CONTINUOUS   96A

Still hearning occasional distant barking, Miles finds
his way among the trees and bushes, looking in vain for
the ill-fated cur.

After a frenetic search, Miles reluctantly gives up and
heads back.

97   **OMIT**   97

98   **EXT. BUCOLIC ROAD - DAY**   98

Miles has returned to where he hit the dog.

Just then, Miles notices TWO MEXICAN CHILDREN watching
him from just down the road. They disappear into the
bushes.

Looking like a criminal, Miles trots back to the Saab,
climbs behind the wheel and speeds away.

99   **EXT. WINDMILL INN - DAY**   99

The Saab pulls into the parking lot.

100   **EXT/INT. MOTEL ROOM - DAY**   100

Miles trudges up the steps to the room. He opens the
door and sees --

JACK
atop Stephanie, plowing her fertile fields. Despite the
interruption, their pace does not alter.

                         JACK
              Not now! Not now!

Miles quickly shuts the door.

101   **INT. WINDMILL SPORTS BAR LOUNGE - DAY**   101

Miles pours himself another glass of Pinot. Jack comes
in and spots his morose friend.

                         JACK
              Hey, there you are.

                        MILES
              Yep.

                         JACK
              What're you drinking?

Jack reaches over to check out the bottle's label. Miles
remains cool to Jack's amiability.

                         JACK (CONT'D)
          Any good?

Miles shrugs.

                         JACK (CONT'D)
                    (to the bartender)
          Could I get a glass please?
                    (to Miles)
          Stephanie took me out into the Pinot
          fields today. It was awesome. I think I
          finally got a handle on the whole
          process, from the soil to the vine to the
          -- what do you call it? -- selection and
          harvest. And the whole, you know, big
          containers where they mix it. We even
          ate Pinot grapes right off the vine.
                    (the new expert)
          Still a little sour but already showing
          potential for great structure. Stephanie
          really knows her shit, Miles.

Jack now has his glass and pours himself some wine.

                         MILES
          Where is Stephanie?

                         JACK
          Upstairs. Getting cleaned up.

                         MILES
          What the fuck are you doing?

                         JACK
          What?

                         MILES
          With this chick.

Jack just looks at him.

                         MILES (CONT'D)
          Does she know about Saturday?

                         JACK
          Um... not exactly. But I've been honest.
          I haven't told her I'm available. And
          she knows this trip up here is only for a
          few days. Besides...

Jack stops short in a rare instance of self-censorship.

                         MILES
          Besides what?

                         JACK
          Well... I don't know, just... the
          wedding.

                         MILES
          What?

                         JACK
          Well, I've been doing some thinking.

                         MILES
          Oh, you've been *thinking*. And?

                         JACK
          I may have to put the wedding on hold is
          all.

Miles looks at him with incredulity.

                         JACK (CONT'D)
          I fully realize that making a change like
          that might be tricky for certain people to
          accept at first, but life is short, Miles.
          I've got to be sure I'm doing the right
          thing before taking such a big step. And
          not just for my sake. I'm thinking about
          Christine's feelings too. I take marriage
          very seriously -- always have. That's why
          I've never done it before. The day I get
          married, it's going to be the real thing.

Miles just looks at his friend, waiting for more.

                         JACK (CONT'D)
          Being with Stephanie has opened my eyes.
          She's not uptight or controlling. She's
          just cool. Things are so easy with her.
          Smells different. Tastes different.
          Fucks different. Fucks like an animal.
          I'm telling you, I went deep last night,
          Miles. Deep.

                         MILES
          Deep.

Miles draws a long sigh.

                         JACK
          Don't get all judgmental on me. This is
          my deal. It's my life, and it's my call.

They fall silent for a moment. Then --

                    JACK (CONT'D)
          I was hoping to get some understanding
          from you. And I'm not getting it.

                    MILES
          Understanding of what?

                    JACK
          Like I might be in love with another
          woman.

                    MILES
          In love? Twenty-four hours with some
          wine-pourer chick and you think you're in
          love? And give up everything?

                    JACK
          Look who's talking. You've been there.

                    MILES
          Yes I have, and do I look like a happy man?
          Was all that drama with Brenda a happy thing
          for me to do? Huh? Was it? Is she a part
          of my life now?

                    JACK
          This is totally different. I'm talking
          about avoiding what you're talking about.
          That's the distinction. I have not made
          the commitment yet. I am not married. I
          have not said the words. In a few days, I
          might get married, and if I do, then I
          won't be doing stuff like this anymore.
          Otherwise, what's the whole point of
          getting married?

                    MILES
          And what about Stephanie? She's a woman --
          with a kid. A single mom. What do you think
          she's looking for? Huh?

                    JACK
                  (interrupting)
          Here's what I'm thinking. We move up here,
          you and me, buy a vineyard. You design
          your own wine; I'll handle the business
          side. Then you get inspired and write a
          new novel. As for me, if an audition comes
          along, hell, LA's two hours away. Not
          even.

                    MILES
          You're crazy. You've gone crazy.

                    JACK
          What do you care anyway? You don't even
          like Christine.

                    MILES
          What? Of course I like Christine.

                    JACK
          You said she was shallow. Yeah, and a
          nouveau riche.

                    MILES
          That was three years ago after that first
          party!

                    JACK
          Look, Miles, all I know is I'm an actor.
          All I have is my instinct.
                    (his hand on his chest)
          My intuition -- that's all I have. And
          you're asking me to go against it. And
          that's just wrong.

Just then Stephanie walks in. She cozies up to Jack, and
he kisses the top of her head.

                    STEPHANIE
          Hi, guys. We should probably get going.

                    MILES
          Where?

102   **INT. BOWLING ALLEY -- DUSK**   102

          CLOSE ON A VIDEO GAME MONITOR
          as a crazy car races through an obstacle-ridden track,
          often leaving the road, much like Jack's libido.

          ZOOM OUT to reveal six-year-old SIENA seated in Jack's lap a
          they drive together. A delighted Siena laughs and giggles.

          Miles sits nearby with Stephanie and her fifty-something,
          two-pack-a-day MOTHER CARYL.

                    CARYL
          Stephanie's heard this a thousand times, but
          if I'd done what I wanted and I'd bought up
          in Santa Maria when I had the chance, I
          would have made a fortune when they put in
          that outlet center and that Home Depot.
                    (a drag off her cigarette,
                    then to Stephanie)
          Your father knew it too, but he was a
          fucking chickenshit. Always was.

Caryl looks over her shoulder, her gaze drawn to Jack and
Siena, so completely happy together.

Caryl exhales a puff of smoke as she watches. Stephanie
is equally enthralled. Miles takes it all in, trying his
best not to shake his head in disgust.

EXT. BOWLING ALLEY PARKING LOT -- DUSK   103

Caryl is behind the wheel of her OLDSMOBILE as Stephanie
gets Siena buckled up in the backseat. Jack pulls Miles
aside.

                    JACK
          Listen, I'm going to make sure Steph and
          Siena get home safe, and then maybe we'll
          hook up with you later, okay?

                    MILES
                    (dispirited)
          Sure, whatever. Maybe I'll catch a
          movie.

Stephanie kisses Miles's cheek before getting in the car
next to her mom.

                    STEPHANIE
          See you, Miles. You take care.

                    MILES
          Bye, Stephanie. Bye, Siena, Caryl.

                    SIENA AND CARYL
          Bye, Miles.

As he gets in the car --

                    JACK
          Call me on my cell if you go out.

                        MILES
            Yeah.

Miles watches them drive away, then heads toward his Saab.

104   **INT. MINI-MART - DUSK**   104

        CLOSE ON THE COUNTER --

        as Miles places a box of security ENVELOPES, a packet of
        BEEF JERKY and some TROPICAL FRUIT SKITTLES.

        WIDE --

        Miles points over the CASHIER'S SHOULDER.

                        MILES
                And could I get a <u>Barely Legal</u>?

        As the cashier reaches for the magazine --

                        MILES (CONT'D)
                No, um, the new one.

105   **INT. MOTEL ROOM BATHROOM - NIGHT**   105

        Miles is once again FLOSSING.

106   **INT. MOTEL ROOM - NIGHT**   106

        POP! Miles opens a bottle of Pinot and pours himself a
        glass. He carries it to the bed, takes a nice big slug,
        lies down on the bed and opens his magazine.

        NOW SNOOZING ATOP THE BED -- ANGLE ON TOP OF HIM --

        The <u>Barely Legal</u> face down on his chest, Miles awakens
        with a start and looks at the clock-radio. He thinks a
        moment, takes a deep breath, and bounds off the bed.

        CLOSE ON A WATER-SAVER SHOWER HEAD --
        as little needles of water come at us.

        THROUGH THE BATHROOM DOOR --

        Miles takes a nice hot SHOWER. But wait -- he has forgotten
        to put the shower curtain inside the tub. A closer look
        reveals a growing PUDDLE OF WATER on the floor.

EXT. THE HITCHING POST - NIGHT   107

Miles walks across the parking lot. He pauses before
entering, then forces himself to take the leap.

INT. THE HITCHING POST - NIGHT   108

Miles affects nonchalance as he searches briefly for Maya.
He continues on into the BAR.

                         GARY
          How's it hanging, Miles?

                         MILES
          You know me. I love it up here. How
          about you?

                         GARY
          Busy night for a Tuesday. We had a busload
          of retired folks in on a wine tour.
          Usually they're not too rowdy, but tonight
          there was something going on. Full moon or
          something. What can I get you?

                         MILES
          Highliner.

                         GARY
          Glass or bottle?

                         MILES
               (considers, then --)
          Bottle.

                         GARY
          You got it.

                         MILES
          Say, is Maya working?

                         GARY
          Maya? Haven't seen her. I think she's
          off tonight. Say, where's your buddy?

Miles just smiles.

WIDE --

Gary serves Miles, alone at the bar. Miles takes his
first drink.

                         MILES
               Oh, that's tasty.

109   **EXT. HITCHING POST - NIGHT**   109

        It's closing time. The front door flies open, and Miles
        staggers out sideways. Gary follows him out, concerned.

                         GARY
               You okay, Miles?

                         MILES
               I'm good.

        Miles heads in the wrong direction at first, then
        realizes his mistake and steers himself back toward the
        Windmill.

                                                      FADE OUT

        UNDER BLACK, A CARD --

                         WEDNESDAY

110   **INT. MOTEL ROOM - DAY**   110

        The door bursts open, and Jack comes bounding in.

                         JACK
               Come on, dude. Let's go golfing! I got
               us in at Alisal.

        Miles comes to, very hungover.

                         MILES
               That's a public course.
                    (then --)
               No Stephanie?

                         JACK
               She's working. I need a break anyway.
               She's getting a little clingy.
                    (magnanimous)
               This is our day!

111   **EXT. GOLF COURSE - DAY**   111

        WHACK! Jack TEES OFF with a manly athletic swing and
        shades his eyes to watch the ball's trajectory.

                    JACK
          Crap.

Miles, disheveled and sullen, approaches the teebox,
sticks a tee in the ground and sets his ball.

                    JACK (CONT'D)
          Did you ever got ahold of Maya yesterday?

                    MILES
          Nope.

                    JACK
          She likes you, man. Stephanie'll tell you.

                    MILES
              (preparing to swing)
          Can you give me some room here?

                    JACK
              (stepping back)
          Oh yeah. Sure.

Miles lifts his club.

                    JACK (CONT'D)
          You know, in life you gotta strike when
          the iron's hot.

                    MILES
          Thanks, Jack.

Miles refocuses and SWINGS just as Jack offers more
helpful advice.

                    JACK
          Don't whiff it.

WHACK! Despite the distraction, Miles manages to make a
good, long drive.

                    JACK (CONT'D)
          Nice shot.

                    MILES
          You're an asshole.

1A   NOW ON THE FAIRWAY --   111A

Jack is pouring two Dixie cups of wine as Miles prepares
to take his next swing.

                    JACK
What about your agent?   Hear anything yet?

                    MILES
Nope.

                    JACK
What do you think's going on?

                    MILES
Could be anything.

                    JACK
Been checking your messages?

                    MILES
Obsessively.

                    JACK
Huh.

                    MILES
They probably think my book is such a
piece of shit that it's not even worthy
of a response.   I guess I'll just have to
learn how to kiss off three years of my
life.

                    JACK
But you don't know yet, so your
negativity's a bit premature, wouldn't
you say?

Miles says nothing.

                    JACK (CONT'D)
Or fuck those New York publishers.
Publish it yourself. I'll chip in.   Just
get it out there, get it reviewed, get it
in libraries. Let the public decide.

Giving Jack a look that says Jack has no idea what he's
talking about, Miles takes a stance over the ball and
focuses.

                    JACK (CONT'D)
Don't come over the top.   Stay still.

                    MILES
Shut up.

                    JACK
          Just trying to be helpful.
               (a moment later)
          It's all about stillness, Miles. Inner
          quiet.

Miles drops his club and turns to Jack.

                    MILES
          Shut up! Shut up! Shut up! What's the
          matter with you, man? SHUT UP!

                    JACK
          Why are you so hostile? I know you're
          frustrated with your life right now, but
          you can choose not to be so hostile.
               (holding out a cup of wine)
          Here.

Still fuming, Miles begrudgingly accepts the wine and has
a taste. He's immediately distracted from his woes.

                    MILES
          What is it?

                    JACK
          I don't know. Got it from Stephanie.

Miles downs the rest and is intrigued by the taste.

                    MILES
          Huh. Let me see the label.

Suddenly a golfball THUDS against the hard fairway
directly behind them.

                    JACK
               (whirling around)
          What the fuck?

Way back on the tee box, some 200 yards away, are a
FOURSOME of two couples. One of the MEN is waving his
driver.

                    HUSBAND #1
               (shouting, barely audible)
          Hurry it up, will you?

Jack looks at Miles, the two incredulous.

                    MILES
          Fucker hit into us.

                    JACK
                  (yelling)
          Hey, asshole! That's not cool!

                    MILES
          Throw me his ball.

Jack walks over, picks up the offending ball and tosses
it to Miles. Miles gets out his 3-wood and -- THWOCK! --
cuts it back low and hard.

                    JACK
          Nice shot.

THE COUPLES
duck for cover as the ball whistles over their heads.

JACK AND MILES
laugh hard.

THE TWO HUSBANDS
climb in their CART and hasten down the fairway toward
Jack and Miles.

JACK
watches their approach, grinning.

                    JACK (CONT'D)
          Oh, this is going to be fun.
                  (jerking a driver from his bag.)
          This is going to be fun.

Jack heads in their direction, brandishing the club like
a medieval knight with a mace.

As the husbands get a look at this sight, they turn their
cart around and speed back toward their wives.

                    JACK (CONT'D)
          Hit into us again, motherfuckers, and
          I'll ass-rape all four of you!

112   **EXT. GOLF COURSE CLUBHOUSE -- DAY**   112

Jack and Miles are turning in their cart and hoisting their
clubs over their shoulders.

                    JACK
          Just don't give up on Maya. Cool smart
          chicks like that -- they like persistence.

                    MILES
          I don't want to talk about it.

                    JACK
          All I know is she's beautiful. Lots of
          soul. Perfect for you. I'm not going to
          feel good about this trip until you guys
          hook up. Don't you just want to feel that
          cozy little box grip down on your Johnson?

Nearby a GOLFER is with his YOUNG SON.

                    GOLFER
          Hey, you mind keeping it down, buddy?

2A   **EXT. GOLF COURSE PARKING LOT - DAY**   112A

Miles and Jack walk toward their car.

                    JACK
          Is it the money thing?

                    MILES
          Is what the money thing?

                    JACK
          With Maya.

                    MILES
          Well, yeah, that's part of it. Woman
          finds out how I live, that I'm not a
          published author, that I'm a liar
          essentially, then yeah, any interest is
          gonna evaporate real quick. If you don't
          have money at my age, you're not even in
          the game. You're just a pasture animal
          waiting for the abattoir.

                    JACK
          Is an abattoir like a... like a... what
          is that?

                    MILES
          Slaughterhouse.

                    JACK
          Abattoir. Huh. But you are going get
          the good news this week about your book.
          I know you are. I can feel it.

Jack's CELLPHONE rings, and he checks the caller ID.

                         JACK (CONT'D)
          It's Steph.
                    (picking up)
          Hey, baby. Yeah. Oh yeah. Yesssss. I
          mean I would, but let me see. Hey,
          Miles... Oh fuck it, we're going. We'll
          be right there. Me. Too.

He snaps his phone shut and turns to Miles.

                         JACK (CONT'D)
          We're on.

                         MILES
          What's happening?

                         JACK
          We're going to have some fun. Remember fun?
          We're going to have some of it. Okay?

                         MILES
          What exactly are we going to do?

                         JACK
          I said okay?

                         MILES
          You have to tell me--

                         JACK
          I SAID OKAY?

Miles finally smiles.

                         MILES
          Okay.

113   **OMITTED**   113

                              BIG FUN MUSIC BEGINS OVER:

114   **EXT. DOWNTOWN LOS OLIVOS - DAY**   114

A HIGH WIDE SHOT --

The Saab pulls up where Stephanie and Maya await with
bottles of wine and a PICNIC BASKET. The girls climb
into the back seat, and the car speeds away.

INT./EXT. THE SAAB - DAY   115

They're going FAST, hair whipping around.

> MAYA
> Hey, Miles, I heard you came by the
> restaurant last night asking for me.

> MILES
> Oh, yeah. No. I mean yeah, I stopped by
> for a drink. Didn't see you.

> MAYA
> I had class.

> MILES
> Well, nice to see you now.

> MAYA
> You too.

EXT. BEAUTIFUL ROAD -- DAY   116

WHOOSH! That car's going a little too FAST!

INT./EXT. LA PURISIMA MISSION CHURCH   117

The two couples wander around this historic site.

EXT. IDYLLIC PICNIC SPOT -- DAY INTO DUSK   118

The girls have led them to a beautiful spot.

IN A SERIES OF SHOTS --
we see the progress of their picnic. We don't hear them,
but there is a growing intimacy about their interaction.
Even Maya and Miles seem to be overcoming residual
awkwardness from the other night. Jack and Stephanie
lean on each other as they eat and sip wine.

Finally, the two couples are SILHOUETTED against the SUNSET.

EXT. WINERY #3 PARKING LOT -- EVENING   119

The parking lot is crowded. The foursome join others
headed toward the main building.

120   **INT. WINERY #3 -- EVENING**   120

A LECTURE by British wine sage LESLIE BROUGH is in progress. He holds aloft a RIEDEL BURGUNDY GLASS containing one of the few but growing number of local reds worthy of his attention.

IN THE AUDIENCE --

As our foursome listen attentively, Jack leans over to Miles.

                JACK
        You ever actually read any of this guy's
        books?

                MILES
        He wrote a great one on Burgundy, and I
        used to get his newsletter, but then
        there were doubts about whether he does
        all his own tasting. Plus a couple of
        times he declared certain years vintages
        of the century, and they turned out to be
        turkeys. Fucker never retracted.

                JACK
    Huh.

Stephanie leans forward and signals to Maya with a YAWN or GAGGING FINGER IN MOUTH that they hightail it. Although Miles protests at first, they stand and leave.

AT THE BACK OF THE ROOM --

Stephanie finds a DOOR which she tests to see whether it is open. It is! She leads her pals furtively inside --

121   **INT. WINEMAKING ROOM - CONTINUOUS**   121

This is an enormous, dimly-lit chamber filled with stainless steel FERMENTATION TANKS and stacks of OAK BARRELS.

As the two couples walk in the near-darkness, they are entranced. Maya takes Miles's hand and leads him away.

LATER --

In the background, Stephanie and Jack lean against a tank, kissing.

CAMERA DOLLIES to reveal Miles and Maya among the barrels in the foreground. They are shy with each other, on the verge of kissing but holding back.

THE MUSIC CONTINUES...

2   **INT. STEPHANIE'S LIVING ROOM - NIGHT**   122

THREE BOTTLES OF WINE
sit empty on the coffee table.

WIDE --

The four friends sit on the floor around the coffee table. They drink wine and pass a JOINT. Suddenly they explode in LAUGHTER.

A sleepy Siena appears at the hallway door rubbing her eyes. Stephanie gets up, but Jack stops her, gathers Siena in his arms, and takes her back to bed.

3   **EXT. STEPHANIE'S HOUSE - NIGHT**   123

The Saab pulls away from the house.

4   **INT. SAAB - NIGHT**   124

Miles sits in his own passenger seat as Maya tries her hand at the Saab.

5   **EXT. MAYA'S APARTMENT BUILDING - NIGHT**   125

Maya leads Miles up her back stairway. They're both a little woozy from the hours of drinking.

AT THE DOOR --

Maya searches through her purse for her keys while Miles hovers directly behind her, staring at her ear. Her ear?

Just as Maya puts the key in the lock, he impulsively leans forward to kiss the nape of her neck. Maya's reaction is immediate -- she turns to embrace Miles, giving him a long KISS. Then she opens the door, pulls him inside and closes the door in our face.

The camera PANS to the nearby ROOFTOPS.

MUSIC ENDS AND SLOW
DISSOLVE TO:

THE SAME VIEW BY DAY, SUPERIMPOSED WITH --

THURSDAY

The CAMERA PANS back to Maya's door, tilting down to find a blue-wrapped NEW YORK TIMES. The door opens, and Maya's hand picks up the newspaper. The CAMERA FOLLOWS Maya inside to --

126   **INT. MAYA'S APARTMENT - CONTINUOUS**   126

It is a small, clean apartment furnished with simple taste.

Maya is dressed in a ROBE and holds a COFFEE MUG. She drops the paper on the dining table and continues into --

THE BEDROOM --

where Miles lies on his stomach DEAD TO THE WORLD. His stubbly face is squished against the mattress and he SNORES lightly.

Maya looks at him for a moment before shaking his foot.

127   **EXT. FARMERS' MARKET - DAY**   127

This is a weekly event in a big PARKING LOT -- organic produce, candles and incense, honey and cider.

Maya and Miles are shopping. Miles carries the bags.

128   **EXT. ORCHARD - DAY**   128

Across from each other at a PICNIC TABLE, and surrounded by the remnants of BREAKFAST, Miles and Maya read the NEWSPAPER. Miles is doing the CROSSWORD PUZZLE.

                              MAYA
                    You guys should stop by the restaurant
                    for lunch today.

                              MILES
                    Great. What's the latest we can get there?

                              MAYA
                    About two-thirty.

                              MILES
                    Okay.

                    MAYA
                 (noticing)
        Did you hear about this Bordeaux tasting
        dinner down in Santa Barbara Saturday
        night? It's a little pricey, but if you
        wanted to go, I'd be into it. Why don't
        you stay through the weekend?

Miles has just figured out a difficult clue. As he
writes it down --

                    MILES
        No, we've got to get back Friday for the
        rehearsal dinner.

                    MAYA
        What rehearsal dinner?

Miles stops writing.

                    MAYA (CONT'D)
        Who's getting married?

INT./EXT. PARKING AREA NEAR THE ORCHARD - DAY   129

Maya leads the way toward the Saab.

                    MAYA
        Were you *ever* going to say anything?

                    MILES
        Of course I was. I mean, just now I
        could have made up some story, but I
        didn't. I told you the truth.

Maya turns to confront Miles with a look of "Give me a
break." Miles reaches out to touch her.

                    MILES (CONT'D)
        Maya.

                    MAYA
                 (jerking away)
        Don't touch me. Just take me home.

INT. SAAB - DAY   130

Miles drives, glancing occasionally at Maya, who stares
straight ahead.

> MILES
> I've told him. I've told him over and
> over, but he's out of control.

> MAYA
> Do you know what he's been saying to her?

> MILES
> He's an actor, so it can't be good.

> MAYA
> Oh, just that he loves her. That she's
> the only woman who has ever really rocked
> his world. How he adores Siena. How he
> wants to move up here and get a place
> with the two of them and commute when he
> has to.

> MILES
> I'm sure he believed every word.

A stony silence.

> MILES (CONT'D)
> Please believe me. I was even on the
> verge of telling you last night, but...

> MAYA
> But you wanted to fuck me first.

> MILES
> Oh, Maya. No.

> MAYA
> Yeah.

131   **EXT. MAYA'S APARTMENT BUILDING - DAY**   131

Miles brings the car to a stop. Maya opens the door and
begins to get out.

> MAYA
> You know, I just spent three years trying
> to extricate myself from a relationship
> that turned out to be full of deception.
> And I've been doing just fine.

> MILES
> And I haven't been with anyone since my
> divorce. This has been a big deal for
> me, Maya -- hanging out with you, and
> last night. I really like you, Maya.
> (MORE)

>   MILES (CONT'D)
> And I'm not Jack. I'm just his... his
> freshman roommate from San Diego State.

Maya wants to let Miles's words reach her, but she can't
just yet.

>   MAYA
> Could I have my paper, please?

Unsure what she wants at first, Miles reaches into the
back seat for the New York Times. He hands it to her and
watches until she goes inside.

EXT. WINDMILL INN - DAY   132

Miles pulls up and parks.

INT. MOTEL ROOM - DAY   133

As Miles enters, a shirtless Jack drops the Barely Legal
and is immediately upon him, grabbing him in a big
BEARHUG. The TV is on, perhaps showing an E! True
Hollywood Story.

>   JACK
> Yo! Yo! Here's my boy! Here's my boy!
> Who's your daddy, boy? Who is yo' daddy?

>   MILES
> Put me down, Jack.

Jack continues his paean to Miles's triumphant night.

>   MILES (CONT'D)
> I said put me down. Jack!

Still gripping Miles in a bearhug, Jack flings the both
of them onto the bed. Now on top on Miles, Jack KISSES
both cheeks.

>   JACK
> I'm so proud of you! Let me love you!

Now they get up off the bed.

>   JACK (CONT'D)
> So tell me everything. Details. I like
> details.

>   MILES
> No.

                        JACK
          What?

                        MILES
          It's private.

                        JACK
          You're kidding, right? Tell me what
          happened, you fucker, or I'll tie your
          dick in a knot.

                        MILES
          Let's leave it alone.

Jack looks at Miles, his face frozen with incomprehension.

                        JACK
          You didn't get any, did you?
                (off Miles's silence)
          You're a homo.

                        MILES
          Just stop, okay? Make something up, and
          that's what happened. Whatever you want.
          Write my confession, and I'll sign it.
          Just stop pushing me all the time! I
          can't take it! You're an infant! This
          is all a big party for you, but not for
          me! This is serious. And you --
          Just... leave me alone, okay? You're
          fucking me up.

                        JACK
          Wow. Okay. Calm down. Sorry.

Miles begins to calm down. Jack grows concerned and
sensitively puts one arm around his friend.

                        JACK (CONT'D)
          Did you have trouble performing? Yeah,
          that's...

                        MILES
          Shut up! Shut up, Jack!

The phone RINGS and both men look at it, silenced by the
ominous sound.

                        MILES (CONT'D)
          Don't answer it.

But Jack is drawn to it as though enticed by a strange
game of Russian roulette.

                    MILES (CONT'D)
          I'm telling you, don't.

Jack picks up the receiver and puts it to his ear.

                    JACK
          Hello? Oh, hey, honey. How you doing?
          Uh-huh. Uh-huh.
                    (mouthing)
          Christine.

Miles lies on his bed and clamps both hands over his ears,
His face is dark with resentment.

                    JACK (CONT'D)
          Listen, honey. Let me call you back.
          Miles and I are in the middle of something.
          No, it's nothing serious -- Miles is just
          having one of his freak-outs. Yeah. Love
          you too. I'll call you right back.

Jack hangs up.

                    MILES
          This whole week has gone sour. It isn't
          turning out like it was supposed to.
                    (deadly serious)
          I want to go home.

                    JACK
          Who's being selfish now?   I'm the one
          getting married. I thought this week was
          supposed to be about me.

                    MILES
          We gotta slow down.
                    (closing his eyes)
          I'm so tired. Let's just get out of
          here.

                    JACK
          I know what you need.

INT. SEARS - DAY   134

Jack watches Miles be fitted for SNEAKERS. A SALES
ASSOCIATE ties Miles's laces.

                    SALES ASSOCIATE
          There you go.

Miles gets up and walks in a circle.

                          MILES
              Do you like them?

                          JACK
              Yeah, they're great. Sporty. They're
              really sporty.

                          MILES
              Are they too sporty?

135   **INT. MALL -- DAY**   135

        The boys exit Sears, Miles wearing his new shoes and
        carrying a PLASTIC BAG with a string handle.

                          JACK
              Feel better?

        Miles shrugs.

                          JACK (CONT'D)
                        (noticing something)
              Oh here, wait a second. I want to run in
              here real quick.

        He heads toward a TOYS STORE.

                          JACK (CONT'D)
                        (over his shoulder)
              I want to get something for Siena.

        Mildly concerned, Miles watches Jack go into the store.

135A   **INT./EXT. SAAB - DAY**   135A

        Miles is slumped in the passenger seat as Jack drives.
        They pass a BIG COMMERCIAL WINERY. Jack slows down,
        preparing to turn in.

                          JACK
              How about this one? We didn't hit this
              one.

                          MILES
              Yeah, it's Frass Canyon. It's a joke.

                          JACK
              You ever actually been in there, Miles?

                          MILES
              I don't have to.

> JACK
> (turning the wheel)
> I say we check it out. You never know.

EXT. LARGE WINERY PARKING LOT - DAY   136

The Saab finds a place in the large parking lot. A TOUR
BUS, whose flank reads "Solvang Wine Tours," is in the
process of letting out WINE TOURISTS, many of them
elderly.

INT. LARGE WINERY - DAY   137

The room boasts not only a large TASTING BAR but also
display after display of t-shirts, golf shirts, olive
oils, chocolate sauces and other gourmet tourist items
emblazoned with the winery's logo.

In the corner an ACOUSTIC GUITARIST with a small amp
plays soothing Windham Hill-ish music.

The tasting bar is packed three-deep with TASTERS
attended to by HARRIED POURERS.

Finally the POURER gets to their glasses. Miles chews a sip
and swallows, then downs the rest in a single gulp.

> MILES
> Tastes like the back of a fucking LA
> schoolbus. Probably didn't de-stem, hoping
> for some semblance of concentration,
> crushed it up with leaves and mice, wound
> up with this rancid tar and turpentine
> mouthwash bullshit. Fucking Raid.

> JACK
> I don't know. Tastes okay to me.
> (looking at the tasting
> sheet)
> Hey, they got a reserve pinot.

> MILES
> Let me use your phone.

> JACK
> (handing it over)
> What's up?

                              MILES
            I can't take it anymore. I've got to
            call Evelyn.

138   **EXT. LARGE WINERY - DAY**   138

       Walking across the lawn outside, Miles holds the
       cellphone to his ear.

                              ASSISTANT (ON THE PHONE)
            Evelyn Berman-Silverman's office.

                              MILES
            Hi, it's Miles.

                              ASSISTANT (ON THE PHONE)
            Oh, hi, Miles. Let me see if I can get her.
                 (a moment later)
            You're in luck. I'll put you through.

                              EVELYN (ON THE PHONE)
            Miles.

                              MILES
            Hey, Evelyn, it's your favorite client.

                              EVELYN (ON THE PHONE)
            How's the trip?

                              MILES
            Good, good. Drinking some good wines and
            kicking back, you know. So what's
            happening? Still no word?

                              EVELYN (ON THE PHONE)
            Actually there is word. I spoke to Keith
            Kurtzman this morning.

                              MILES
            And?

                              EVELYN (ON THE PHONE)
            And... they're passing. Conundrum's
            passing. He said they really liked it.
            They really wanted to do it, but they
            just couldn't figure out how to market
            it. He said it was a really tough call.

                              MILES
            Huh.

                    EVELYN (ON THE PHONE)
          I'm sorry, Miles.
                    (off his silence)
          So I don't know where that leaves us.
          I'm not sure how much more mileage I can
          get out of continuing to submit it. I
          think it's one of those unfortunate cases
          in the business right now -- a fabulous
          book with no home. The whole industry's
          gotten gutless. It's not about the
          quality of the books. It's only about
          the marketing.

Miles is at a loss for words. A distant RUMBLE begins to
sound, the familiar harbinger of an anxiety attack.

EXT. DEEP CANYON - INSERT   139

Once again we see the narrow ROPE BRIDGE extending
vertiginously across a great CHASM.

EXT. LARGE WINERY - BACK AGAIN   140

                    EVELYN (ON THE PHONE)
          Are you there? Miles?

                    MILES
          Yeah, I'm here.

                    EVELYN (ON THE PHONE)
          I'm sorry, Miles. We did all we could.
          You've been a real trooper.
                    (loudly, to her assistant)
          Tell him I'll call back.

                    MILES
          So I guess that's it.

                    EVELYN (ON THE PHONE)
          You're a wonderful writer, Miles. Don't
          be discouraged.

MOMENTS LATER --

Miles STAGGERS toward the tasting room, unpocketing his
Xanax and downing a couple, as Evelyn's clichés of
consolation continue in his head.

                        EVELYN (ON THE PHONE) (CONT'D)
         Just hang in there, and who knows? After
         you get something else published, we can
         revisit this one. And next time we can
         try a different title.

Once back at the tent, he leans against it in a vain
attempt to steady himself. The RUMBLE grows deafening.

141   **INT. LARGE WINERY -- DAY**   141

Now inside, Miles grabs the first DIRTY WINE GLASS he finds
and shakes it out as he approaches the closest tasting
station. He pushes his way to front.

The pourer offers the usual one-ounce dollop. Miles
jacks it back, immediately extending his glass for more.

                        MILES
         Hit me again.

The same small amount is poured and downed. Once again
Miles holds out his glass.

                        MILES (CONT'D)
         Pour me a full glass. I'll pay for it.

                        POURER
         This is a tasting, sir. Not a bar.

Miles slams a TWENTY-DOLLAR BILL on the table.

                        MILES
         Just give me a full goddamn pour.

The pourer turns away to serve another party. Miles
looks around indignantly, as though everyone should be
sympathetic to this injustice.

Now Miles boldly reaches over and pours himself a glass
right up to the brim and beyond.

                        POURER
         Sir, what are you doing?

                        MILES
         I told you I need a drink.

                        POURER
         Then buy a bottle and go outside.

The pourer grabs Miles by the wrist before he can drink.

> POURER (CONT'D)
> Put the glass down.

In the ensuing struggle, the wine spills, and everyone nearby steps back.

> POURER (CONT'D)
> You're going to have to leave, sir.

The pourer signals to a SECURITY GUY at the door. Across the room Jack notices the disturbance and heads over.

Miles hoists up the SPIT BUCKET, holds it aloft and starts to GUZZLE IT. Wine cascades down the sides of his face, onto his shirt and even onto his shiny new shoes.

The Security Guy yanks the bucket away from Miles, and drags him toward the EXIT. Jack catches up.

> JACK
> (to the horrified onlookers)
> It's all right. His mother just died.

EXT. BEACH - DAY   142

TWO PELICANS soar low over the water. One of them DIVES, crashing into the water and disappearing from view.

Jack and Miles sit on the hood of the Saab, gazing at the ocean, sharing a bottle of wine.

> JACK
> Just write another one. You have lots of ideas, right?

> MILES
> No, I'm finished. I'm not a writer. I'm a middle-school English teacher. I'm going to spend the rest of my life grading essays and reading the works of others. It's okay. I like books. The world doesn't give a shit what I have to say. I'm unnecessary.
> (a dark laugh)
> I'm so insignificant, I can't even kill myself.

> JACK
> What's that supposed to mean?

                    MILES
You know -- Hemingway, Sexton, Woolf,
Plath, Delmore Schwartz. You can't kill
yourself before you've even been
published.

                    JACK
What about that guy who wrote <u>Confederacy
of Dunces</u>? He committed suicide before
he got published, and look how famous he
is.

                    MILES
Thanks.

                    JACK
Don't give up. You're going to make it.

                    MILES
Half my life is over, and I have nothing to
show for it. I'm a thumbprint on the
window of a skyscraper. I'm a smudge of
excrement on a tissue surging out to sea
with a million tons of raw sewage.

                    JACK
See? Right there. Just what you just
said. That's beautiful. A thumbprint on
a skyscraper. I couldn't write that.

                    MILES
Neither could I. I think it's Bukowski.

Unable to respond, Jack looks up and down the beach.

143   **EXT. BUCOLIC ROAD -- DAY**   143

ZOOM! There goes the Saab.

The CAMERA lingers behind and PANS to reveal THE DEAD DOG,
now covered with FLIES AND MAGGOTS.

144   **EXT. WINDMILL INN - DAY**   144

Jack and Miles pull into the parking lot.

                    JACK
                 (lighting up)
        Oh, look. There's Steph!

He smiles broadly and honks his horn. Miles turns to see --

STEPHANIE
seated halfway up the motel stairs, her HELMET in her
lap, watching patiently as --

THE SAAB
pulls to a stop in a parking space.

Miles masks his concern as he gets out of the car and
reaches in the backseat for his Sears bag.

                    JACK (CONT'D)
                 (calling out)
           Hey, baby.

Stephanie stands up and slowly descends the steps, as
Jack reaches into the trunk and pulls out a BIG CUDDLY
LION DOLL.

                    JACK (CONT'D)
           Look what I got for our favorite girl.

Stephanie walks toward Jack as he waddles toward her
hugging the lion. When they get close, Stephanie's face
transforms with rage.

                    STEPHANIE
           YOU MOTHERFUCKER!

She swings her helmet and HITS JACK FULL IN THE FACE.

Jack falls, blood spraying out of his nose. Stephanie stands
over him and continues to BEAT HIM with her helmet as he rolls
back and forth, protecting his head with the stuffed lion.

Miles ineffectually attempts to stop her, dancing just
out of range.

                    MILES
           Stephanie! Stop!

                    STEPHANIE
           You fucking bastard! Lying piece of shit!
           You're getting married on Saturday? What
           was all that shit you said to me?

                    JACK
           I can explain.

                    STEPHANIE
           You said you loved me! You fuck! I hope you die!

With that she backs away. Glancing at her bloodied helmet,
she tosses it onto the pavement before getting on her bike.

STEPHANIE (CONT'D)
Fuckface!
          (to Miles)
You too!

As she speeds away, Miles is left to comfort his wounded
friend. The lion lies nearby, staring blankly at the sky.

145   **INT./EXT. SAAB - DAY**   145

Seated in the passenger seat and in great agony, Jack
presses a BLOOD-SOAKED TOWEL against his face.

                    MILES
          Aren't you glad you didn't move up here
          and marry her?

                    JACK
          Don't need a lecture. You fucking told
          Maya, didn't you?

                    MILES
          No, I did not. Must have been Gary at the
          Hitching Post. I think we mentioned it to
          him the first night.

                    JACK
          You told him. I'm fucking hurting here.

                    MILES
          Keep it elevated.

146   **INT. HOSPITAL ER WAITING ROOM - DAY**   146

CLOSE ON A COSMOPOLITAN
open to an article titled "24 Ways To Please Your Man."

WIDER --

Miles reads, while nearby a YOUNG BOY dry-heaves into a
garbage can held by his FATHER. An OLD WOMAN parked in a
wheelchair faces the wall.

LATER --

Miles is at a PAYPHONE. As he speaks he tries to peel
off the metal LONG DISTANCE STICKER.

                    MAYA (ON THE PHONE)
          Hi. It's Maya. Please leave a message.

                    MILES
It's Miles. Listen, I don't know if you even
care, but I had to call and tell you again how
much I enjoyed our time together and how sorry
I am things turned out the way they did. I
think you're great, Maya -- always have. From
the first time you waited on me.
          (bracing himself)
And while I'm at it, I guess you should
know that my book is not getting
published. I thought this one had a
chance, but I was wrong. Again. Don't
bother reading it -- you've got better
things to do. So you see I'm not much of
a writer. I'm not anything really. The
only real talent I seem to have is for
disappointing people and now you know
that firsthand. We're leaving in the
morning, and I want you to know that I
take with me wonderful memories of you.
I'm sorry. I'm really sorry.

What else to say? He hangs up.

He returns to his seat. A moment later he extends his
legs to look at his new SHOES now STAINED WITH WINE.

LATER --

Jack emerges unsteadily from the bowels of the emergency
room, his face purple and swollen beneath the HUGE WHITE
BANDAGE that holds the NOSEGUARD in place. Miles walks
with him toward the exit.

                    MILES (CONT'D)
Well?

                    JACK
I'm going to need an operation. Maybe a
couple of them. They have to wait for it
to heal first. Then they break it again.

                    MILES
Good thing you have a voice-over career.

                    JACK
Gonna fuck that up too. I should sue her
ass. Only reason I won't is to protect
Christine.

                    MILES
That's thoughtful.

                              JACK
                        (disgusted)
              Yeah.

They walk by us and out the door.

147   **EXT. STREET IN SOLVANG - DAY**   147

Jack sits in the Saab's passenger side with the seat almost
fully reclined. When his agony allows him to open his
eyes, he glares at the DANISH THEMED STORES lining the
street. An ABELSKIVER MAKER plies his lofty trade in a
nearby window.

He hears a strange CLOMPING NOISE and turns his head to
see a MAN IN WOODEN CLOGS walking noisily down the
street, dressed in a TRADITIONAL DANISH COSTUME and
carrying a TUBA. Jack takes a slug of wine.

Just then Miles gets back in the car.

                              JACK
              I hate this place.

Miles tears open a paper bag and removes a bottle of
pills. A closer angle reveals them as VICODIN.

                              MILES
              Take a couple of these, and you'll learn
              to love it.

Miles opens the bottle and hands Jack two PILLS.

                          MILES (CONT'D)
              Two for you. And two for me.

Jack washes down the pills and passes the bottle to
Miles, who follows suit.

148   **EXT. WINDMILL INN JACUZZI - EVENING**   148

Jack and Miles sit across from each other. For the first
time we see LARGE PURPLE BRUISES on Jack's arms and chest.

                              JACK
              So how did Stephanie know it was Saturday?
              We didn't get into that with Gary.

                              MILES
              Huh. Let me think.

                    JACK
        You sure you didn't say anything to Maya?

                    MILES
        Sure I'm sure. And just what are you
        implying? I'm really pissed off at you
        about all this, if you want to know the
        truth. What's Maya going to think of me
        now just for associating with you?
        You're the one who's sabotaging me, not
        the other way around, pal. Not by a
        longshot.

Jack takes a long lie-detecting look at Miles.

                    JACK
        I don't know. Just seems fishy.

INT. MOTEL ROOM - NIGHT   149

The boys lie on their respective beds staring at the TV.
Jack gets up and lumbers slowly to the dresser MIRROR
like a large dog who has just been neutered.

                    JACK
        What's it look like to you?

                    MILES
        Looks like you were in a bad car accident.

Jack turns to Miles, nodding and thinking. Then he looks
back in the mirror.

                    JACK
        I'm hungry.

EXT. A.J. SPURS BARBECUE - NIGHT   150

Establishing. Thursday night is Cajun Wings Night.

INT. A.J. SPURS BARBECUE - NIGHT   151

Miles and Jack are finishing their SALADS in the rustic-
themed restaurant festooned with animal trophies.

                    JACK
        You know what I'm thinking?

                    MILES
        What's that?

                              JACK
             I'm thinking it's time to settle down. One
             woman. One house. You know. It's time.

                              MILES
                  Uh-huh.

Jack nods his head with no self-awareness or
acknowledgement of the irony.

NOW TWO PLATES ARRIVE
mounded high with ribs, slaw, beans and butter-whipped
mashed potatoes.

                              JACK
                  Mm. Mm.

Their cheery, zaftig blonde WAITRESS removes several FOIL
PACKETS from her apron and places them on the table.

                              WAITRESS
                  And here're your Handi-wipes.

                              JACK
                  Oh, so that's what those are? For a
                  second there I thought you guys were
                  promoting safe sex.

The waitress OVER-LAUGHS and swipes a hand at her naughty
customer.

                              WAITRESS
                  I'll be right back with more corn bread.

Jack watches her go and leans in close to Miles.

                              JACK
                  I bet you that chick is two tons of fun.
                  You know, the grateful type.

                              MILES
                  I don't know. I wouldn't know.

Now she comes back toward the table carrying a BIG
BASKET. Beneath the hideous uniform, her nylons SH-SH-SH
as she walks. When she arrives, she replenishes their
corn bread basket using big TONGS. Jack watches
attentively.

                              JACK
                  Nice technique there...
                       (checking her name tag)
                  ...Cammi.

                         CAMMI
          It's all in the wrist.
                    (a moment later)
          You know, you look really familiar. You
          from around here? Where'd you go to high
          school?

                         JACK
          No, we're from San Diego. Why?

                         CAMMI
          I don't know. You just seem really
          familiar to me. Never mind. Enjoy your
          meals.

                         JACK
          Hang on. Did you ever know a Derek
          Sommersby?

                         CAMMI
          <u>Doctor</u> Derek Sommersby? You mean from
          "One Life to Live?"

Miles looks away and sighs.

                         JACK
          You have to imagine him with a bandage
          and shorter hair.

As Cammi stares at Jack, her face transforms in
astonishment.

                         CAMMI
          No. Way. No way!

Jack smiles and nods.

                         CAMMI (CONT'D)
          Oh, my God!

                         MILES
          Could you tell me where the bathroom is?

                         CAMMI
                    (her eyes barely leaving Jack)
          Uh, sure, it's right over there, right
          past the buffalo.

IN A WIDE SHOT --

Miles gets up and heads toward the bathroom as Jack's
flirtation with Cammi continues.

The camera PANS with Miles as he walks by us and goes
through the bathroom door, which closes behind him,
filling the frame with the word "MEN."

LATER --

A TOOTHPICK DISPENSER
as a finger tips it forward to dispense one.

WIDER --

Miles stands by the cash register and PICKS HIS TEETH as he
watches Jack finish speaking with Cammi and head his way.

> JACK
> She gets off in an hour, so I think I'm
> just going to have a drink and then...
> make sure she gets home safe.

> MILES
> You're joking, right?
> (seeing that he isn't)
> What are you doing? Un-fucking-believable.
> Can't we just go back to the hotel and hang
> out and get up early and play nine holes
> before we head home?

Jack rests one hand on Miles's shoulder and drops his
head, thinking how best to put it.

> JACK
> Look, Miles. I know you're my friend and
> you care about me. And I know you
> disapprove. I respect that. But there
> are some things I have to do that you
> don't understand. You understand wine and
> literature and movies, but you don't
> understand my plight. And that's okay.

CLOSE ON MILES --
as the disappointment in his friend deepens by the
moment.

FADE TO BLACK

UNDER BLACK, SUPERIMPOSED --

FRIDAY

Now comes the sound of hysterical KNOCKING.

2   **INT. MOTEL ROOM -- DAWN**   152

Despite the knocking, Miles remains motionless in bed,
his expression serene.

Finally he awakens and drags himself toward the door,
opening it to find --

JACK
silhouetted against the first rosy fingers of dawn. He
is barefoot. In fact he is clad only in his UNDERWEAR.
Hugging himself, he PANTS and SHIVERS.

                    JACK
          Jesus fucking Christ, it's freezing.

He limps past Miles, yanks off the bed covers and wraps
them around himself.

                    JACK (CONT'D)
          Vicodin. Where's the Vicodin? My nose.

Miles hands him the bottle, and Jack frantically pops a
couple of pills, chewing them like candy. He sits down
and bends over at the waist as though preparing for an
airplane crash.

                    JACK (CONT'D)
          Fucking chick's married.

                    MILES
          What?

                    JACK
          Her husband works a night shift or
          something, and he comes home, and I'm on
          the floor with my cock in his wife's ass.

                    MILES
          Jesus, Jack. Jesus. And you walked all
          the way back from Solvang?

                    JACK
          Ran. Twisted my ankle too.

                    MILES
          That's five clicks, Jackson.

                    JACK
          Fucking-a it's five clicks! At one point I
          had to cut through an ostrich farm. Fuckers
          are mean.

Miles has now awakened enough to take in the absurdity of the
whole scene, and he LAUGHS HARD. The blanketed bulge just
sits there. Finally it looks up and shows its pitiful visage

                    JACK (CONT'D)
          We gotta go back.

                    MILES
          What?

                    JACK
          I left my wallet. My credit cards, cash,
          fucking ID, everything. We gotta go
          back.

                    MILES
          Big deal. We'll call right now and
          cancel your cards.

                    JACK
          You don't understand. The wedding bands.
          The wedding bands are in my wallet.

                    MILES
          Okay, so they were in your wallet, and
          you left your wallet somewhere. Some
          bar. Christine'll understand.

                    JACK
          No. She ordered them special. Took her
          forever to find them. They've got this
          design on them with dolphins and our names
          engraved in Sanskrit. We've got to go
          back. Christine'll fucking crucify me.

                    MILES
          No way. No way.

                    JACK
               (a pitiful whine)
          Please, Miles, please.

                    MILES
          Forget it. Your wallet was stolen at a
          bar. Happens every day.

Jack stares straight ahead, breathing through his mouth
as he considers this. Then --

                    JACK
          No, we've got to get my wallet! Those rings
          are irreplaceable! We've got to get them,
          Miles! I fucked up!
               (MORE)

> JACK (CONT'D)
> I know I fucked up, okay? I fucked up. You
> gotta help me. You gotta help me. Pleeeease!

Jack now descends to a level of wretchedness and
desperation that Miles has never seen before in Jack, or
in anyone else for that matter.

> JACK (CONT'D)
> Oh, God, please... Oh, God. I know I'm
> bad. I know I did a bad thing. Help me,
> Miles. Just this one thing, this one
> last thing. I can't lose Christine. I
> can't. I'm nothing without her. Please,
> Miles, please.... uuuuu.... uuuuuu....
> uuuuuuu......

No longer able to form words, Jack is reduced to emitting
low, primitive sounds. Snot flows from beneath his
bandaged nose.

INT./EXT. SAAB - MORNING   153

Miles drives in the early-morning light. Jack is now
subdued, quieted by his pain and exhaustion.

> MILES
> She tell you she was married?

> JACK
> Yeah.

> MILES
> So what the fuck were you thinking?

> JACK
> Wasn't supposed to be back till six.
> Fucker rolls in at five.

> MILES
> Cutting it a little close, don't you
> think?
>   (off Jack's silence)
> So how was she? Compared to Stephanie,
> say.

> JACK
> Horny as shit. Flopping around like a
> landed trout.

EXT. LOW-RENT STREET - MORNING   154

The Saab creeps around a corner.

155   **INT./EXT. SAAB - MORNING**   155

Jack scans the street.

> JACK
> Yeah, this is the block. Just keep
> going...
>> (spotting an AMC Pacer)
> Yeah! This is it. There's her car.

Miles pulls over and cuts the engine.

> MILES
> So what's the plan?

> JACK
> The plan is... you go.

> MILES
> Me?

> JACK
> My ankle. Just go explain the situation.

> MILES
>> (sarcastic, clearing his
>> throat)
> Uh, excuse me, sir, but my friend was the
> one balling your wife a couple hours ago,
> and he seems to have left his wallet
> behind, and we were wondering...

> JACK
> Yeah, yeah. Like that. Just like that.

Miles gives Jack a withering look. Jack reaches for the
the DOOR HANDLE.

> JACK (CONT'D)
> Fuck you. I'll get it myself.

> MILES
>> (grabbing Jack's shirt)
> Hold on.

156   **EXT. CAMMI'S STREET - MORNING**   156

Miles crosses the street and approaches --

57

EXT. CAMMI'S HOUSE-- MORNING   157

Miles presses his ear against the front door. Nothing.
Then he notices --

A SLIDING GLASS DOOR
a few feet away, just barely cracked open.

MILES
creeps over, sticks his hand into the open space and
pulls back the curtain to reveal --

A LIVING ROOM
that is hideously MESSY. Draped over a deformed beanbag
chair are JACK'S LEVI'S.

Miles gathers his courage, carefully slides open the
glass door, and creeps inside.

58

INT. CAMMI'S HOUSE -- CONTINUOUS   158

A furtive search of Jack's pockets reveals NOTHING. Then
Miles notices a HIGH-PITCHED SOUND wafting from an open
door down a short HALLWAY.

Miles feverishly begins foraging through the debris on
the floor. Again nothing. Meanwhile the noise from the
bedroom grows louder -- female MOANING in odd rhythmic
unison with a MAN'S VOICE.

IN THE HALLWAY --

Miles gets on ALL FOURS and starts crawling, weaving his
way through a trail of shoes and clothes.

Nearing the open door, the sounds grow more distinct --

                    MAN
          You don't think I fuck you, bitch? I'll
          fuck you.

                    CAMMI
          I'm a bad girl. I'm a bad girl.

Miles peers around the corner of the open door to see --

159   **INT. CAMMI'S BEDROOM -- CONTINUOUS**   159

Cammi is TIED to the faux brass headboard. A BIG GUY
slams away at her. In the corner a soundless TV shows a
PRESIDENTIAL PRESS CONFERENCE.

                    MAN
          You picked him up and you fucked him,
          didn't you, bitch?

                    CAMMI
          I picked him up and I fucked him. I'm a
          bad girl.

                    MAN
          And you liked fucking him, didn't you,
          you fat little whore?

                    CAMMI
          I liked it when you caught me fucking
          him.

Whoa!

Miles manages to tear his eyes away from this nature
documentary and scan the room.

IRIS IN -- to the WALLET atop the dresser.

Miles's eyes dart back and forth between the couple and
the wallet. His HEART BEATING LOUDLY, he goes for it.
He scrambles to his feet, dashes across the room, seizes
the wallet and tears out. Behind him he hears --

                    MAN (O.S.)
              The fuck was that?

                    CAMMI (O.S.)
              The wallet! He took Derek's wallet!

160   **EXT. CAMMI'S HOUSE - CONTINUOUS**   160

Miles comes flying out of the sliding glass door,
followed swiftly by the man, who is of course STARK
NAKED. And he's fast for a man his size.

                    CAMMI (O.S.)
          Get him!

INT. SAAB - MORNING 161

Jack is reclined in the passenger seat FAST ASLEEP. On the
radio NPR'S CARL KASSEL reads the news.

THROUGH THE DRIVER'S WINDOW --

Miles comes sprinting toward us, mere steps ahead of Cammi's
naked husband. Finding the car door locked, Miles knocks
loudly on the glass, startling Jack awake.

                    MILES
          Open up! Jesus! Open the goddamn door!

Jack flips the electric locks just in time for Miles to
get in before --

WHUMP! The guy's BELLY hits the window. He pounds on
the roof before trying the door, now re-locked.

                    MAN
          You motherfuckers! I'll kill you! I'll
          kill you motherfuckers!

Miles starts the car and begins to drive away. The guy
tries to keep up but can't, running barefoot on asphalt.
Jack turns to look --

OUT THE BACK WINDOW --

The guy recedes in the distance.

JACK
removes the rings from the wallet.

                    JACK
          You did it. You fucking did it!

They LAUGH and SLAP HANDS.

CLOSE ON MILES --
For all his failures, this time he did something right.

INT. MOTEL ROOM - DAY 162

The shades are drawn. Jack is CRASHED OUT on the bed,
snoring loudly. Miles folds his shirts and trousers --
readying his bags for departure.

At one moment he stops and watches his friend sleep.

A KNOCK at the door. Miles goes to answer it, but once his hand is on the knob, he pauses. If we're perceptive, we will know he's hoping against hope that it's Maya.

He opens it. It's just the MAID with her big CART.

MAID
Housekeeping.

163 OMIT 163

164 EXT. 101 FREEWAY - DAY 164

The Saab enters the freeway and heads south.

165 INT./EXT. SAAB - DAY 165

Miles drives while Jack stares out the window, WATCHING THE LANDSCAPE CHANGE as they leave wine country.

MILES
Hey, Jack. Jack.

JACK
Hmmm?

MILES
That was quite a day yesterday.

Jack's eyes close, but his lips spread into a smile.

JACK
Yep. Quite a day.

MILES
Quite a week.

166 EXT. 101 FREEWAY - DAY 166

A driving shot.

167 EXT. FILLING STATION - DAY 167

Miles pumps the gas, while nearby Jack stretches his legs. As Miles puts the nozzle back in place --

JACK
Want me to drive?

MILES
No, I'm okay.

JACK
Hey, why don't you invite Maya to the
wedding?

MILES
Somehow I don't think inviting Maya to your
wedding is the right move. In fact, after
your bullshit, it's going to be hard for me
to even go to the Hitching Post again.

JACK
You're so negative.

Miles replaces the hose and screws on the gas cap.

JACK (CONT'D)
Come on, let me drive.

MILES
I'm fine. You rest.

JACK
I feel like driving.

INT. SAAB -- DAY 168

As the car makes its way back toward the freeway, Jack
looks over at Miles and slows the car to a stop.

MILES
What's wrong?

JACK
Nothing. Buckle up, okay?

Miles obeys. Without hesitation, Jack accelerates and
JUMPS THE CURB, heading into --

EXT. VACANT LOT - CONTINUOUS 169

The Saab plows INTO A TREE.

INT. SAAB - CONTINUOUS 170

MILES
What the fuck!

                    JACK
              (pointing at his face)
          You said it looked like a car accident.

                    MILES
          What the fuck!

                    JACK
          I'll pay for it.

171   **EXT. VACANT LOT - DAY**   171

     They get out to inspect the damage. The hood is slightly
     crumpled, and the front fender is bent.

                    MILES
          Look at this!

                    JACK
          I don't know. Doesn't look like anybody
          got hurt in this one.

                    MILES
          Oh, no. Oh, Christ. No, you don't.

                    JACK
          You need a new car anyway.

     Miles looks at his friend, incredulous.

                    JACK (CONT'D)
          I said I'd pay for it.

     MOMENTS LATER --

     The trunk is open, and the guys are unloading their cases
     of wine. Miles notices that one box is DRIPPING.

                    MILES
          You broke some.

                    JACK
          Whatever. Sorry.

                    MILES
          No, not whatever. You fucking derelict.

     MOMENTS LATER --

     Miles looks on as Jack hoists a FOUNDATION BLOCK toward
     the open driver's door of the Saab.

129.

                         JACK
              You ready?

Miles waves his hand in a gesture of "Get it over with."

Grunting with effort, Jack leans inside the car and drops
the foundation block onto the GAS PEDAL.

Direct hit! Jack leaps backward and hits the dirt just
in time.

Miles and Jack watch the driverless Saab race toward the
tree, its speed increasing. But just before hitting it,
the car drifts to one side and SAILS RIGHT PAST.

                         MILES
              Oh, fuck!

The car zooms wildly across the vacant lot and, missing
the tree, continues on until CRASHING THROUGH A FENCE and
finally toppling headlong into a CEMENT TRENCH. Only the
back of the car remains visible.

The whole thing is finished in a matter of seconds.
Still frozen in place, Miles and Jack turn slowly to each
other.

                         JACK
              It's okay. I've got Triple A.

EXT. 101 FREEWAY - DAY   172

From in front of the Saab, we see its now CRUMPLED HOOD
and FENDER, a couple of BUNGEE CORDS holding the whole
thing together.

EXT. PALOS VERDES STREET -- DAY   173

The Saab approaches the end of the line.

EXT. ERGANIAN HOUSE -- DAY   174

AT THE FRONT PORCH --

Miles has helped Jack carry his bags and the wine. He
plops the last case down.

                         MILES
              Well. That about does it.

>   JACK
>   Why don't you come in?

>   MILES
>   Uh-uh. You're on your own.

>   JACK
>   So I'll see you at the rehearsal.

>   MILES
>   Yeah.

They give each other a brief manly back-slappy HUG.

>   JACK
>   Love you, man.

>   MILES
>   Back at you.

Miles heads toward the curb.

>   JACK
>   Hey, don't pull away till they see the
>   car.

>   MILES
>   (over his shoulder)
>   Yeah.
>   (turning around)
>   Hey, why wasn't I injured?

>   JACK
>   (big smile)
>   You were wearing your belt.

BACK AT HIS CAR --

Miles gets in and watches through the side window as Mrs.
Erganian opens the front door and welcomes Jack with
shock and dismay. Jack points back at --

MILES --
raising one hand in a feeble wave. The camera slowly
MOVES CLOSER as he continues to watch --

JACK --
weaving his story of woe. He's a great actor when he
wants to be. Mr. Erganian and a mortified Christine come
to the door too. Mr. Erganian takes a few steps toward
the car to get a better look.

VERY CLOSE ON MILES --

watching the drama play out. Then his eyes drop as he
momentarily loses himself in melancholy. This reverie is
interrupted by --

THE VOICE OF AN ARMENIAN PRIEST

Startled, Miles turns to look at --

A PRIEST
who is singing the BLESSING OF THE RINGS.

We are now in --

INT. ARMENIAN APOSTOLIC CHURCH - DAY   175

The church is packed.

CLOSE ON THE RINGS as the priest holds them aloft. If
those rings could talk...

Jack shoots a quick look at Miles, who looks right back.

The priest continues his blessing.

EXT. ARMENIAN CHURCH - DAY   176

AT THE TOP OF THE STAIRS --

The WEDDING FAMILIES greet the exiting guests in a
RECEIVING LINE. Smiling and exuberant, Jack seems
utterly at home as the new groom.

AT THE BOTTOM OF THE STEPS --

Miles watches the scene, not without melancholy. Then --

                    VICTORIA (O.S.)
          Hey, Miles.

Miles turns and looks up to see Victoria, standing one step
above him. Just behind her is her NEW HUSBAND. He exudes
the quiet confidence of a successful businessman who played
college football, takes expensive skiing and sailing
vacations, and hasn't read a novel since high school.

                    MILES
          Hi, Vicki.
               (taking her in)
          You look beautiful.

                    VICTORIA
          Thanks. Um, this is Ken Cortland, my
          husband.

From his spot hovering over Miles, Ken leans down and
offers his hand.

                    KEN
          How are you?

                    MILES
          Hi. How you doing? You're a lucky guy.

                    KEN
          Thanks.
               (to Victoria)
          I'll wait for you at the car.
               (to Miles)
          Nice to meet you, Miles.

                    MILES
          Ken.

Exit Ken.

                    MILES (CONT'D)
          That was big of him.

                    VICTORIA
          Yeah, he's good that way. Very
          considerate.

                    MILES
          That's great.

                    VICTORIA
          So how're you doing?

                    MILES
          Since the last time we spoke? I don't
          know. Could be better. Could be worse.

                    VICTORIA
          So what's happening with your book?

                    MILES
          Universally rejected. Strike three.

                    VICTORIA
          Oh, Miles. That's awful. What are you
          going to do?

                    MILES
          Back to the drawing board, I guess. Or not.
          So... you're married. Congratulations. You
          look happy.

                    VICTORIA
          I am.

                    MILES
          Seems like everyone's getting married. A
          year ago it was all divorces. Now it's
          all weddings. Cyclical, I guess.

                    VICTORIA
          I guess.

Just then a BLACK LINCOLN NAVIGATOR pulls up alongside
the curb. The passenger side window is halfway down, and
the sounds of Adult Contemporary Jazz waft out. Victoria
gives Ken a little wave.

                    MILES
                (shifting gears)
          Well, let's go have some champagne, shall
          we? Toast all the newlyweds.

                    VICTORIA
          Not me. I'm not drinking.

                    MILES
          You quit drinking?

                    VICTORIA
          I'm pregnant.

                    MILES
                (hit in the solar plexus)
          Oh. Huh. Well...
                (rallying)
          Congratulations again, Vicki. That's
          wonderful news.

                    VICTORIA
                (going to the car)
          See you over there, Miles.

                    MILES
          Yeah.

As she gets in the car and cruises away, Miles glances
back at --

THE RECEIVING LINE

-- where Mike Erganian is introducing Jack to some dear
old FRIENDS. Mike throws a loving arm around his new son-
in-law, and Jack is drawn into Mike's bosom.

177   **EXT. STREET - DAY**   177

A HAND-PRINTED SIGN, attached to a STOP SIGN and
decorated with balloons, reads: "RECEPTION THIS WAY!"
with an arrow pointing RIGHT.

One by one, CARS are making a right turn. But when his
turn comes, Miles turns LEFT.

178   **EXT. MILES'S APARTMENT COMPLEX - DAY**   178

The Saab pulls up outside. Miles leaves the car idling
as he sprints inside. Moments later he sprints back to
his car, this time carrying SOMETHING.

179   OMIT   179

180   **INT. FAST FOOD PLACE - DAY**   180

His bowtie undone, Miles sits at a booth eating. He
washes down a bite by draining the contents of a big wax-
coated soft-drink cup.

He brings the cup to his lap and refills it from a BOTTLE
OF WINE hidden next to him. As he sets the bottle back
down, we glimpse the label: 1961 Cheval Blanc.

He takes another sip. As the camera MOVES CLOSER, all
the complex emotions inspired by the wine ripple across
Miles's face.

                    14-YEAR-OLD BOY (O.S.)
            "The marrow of his bone," I repeated
            aimlessly. This at least penetrated my
            mind. Phineas had died from the marrow
            of his bone flowing down his blood stream
            to his heart.

181   **INT. MIDDLE SCHOOL CLASSROOM - DAY**   181

The voice belongs to one of Miles's PUPILS reading aloud
in class. Other students follow along silently from
their own copies of <u>A Separate Peace</u>.

SUPERIMPOSED --

FIVE WEEKS LATER

Miles sits behind his desk at the front of the class.

> 14-YEAR-OLD BOY
> I did not cry then or ever about Finny.
> I did not cry even when I stood watching
> him being lowered into his family's
> straight-laced burial ground outside of
> Boston. I could not escape a feeling
> that this was my own funeral, and you do
> not cry in that case.

The students look up.

> 14-YEAR-OLD BOY (CONT'D)
> Do you want me to keep reading the next
> chapter, Mr. Raymond?

> MILES
> (as though coming to)
> Hmmm? No, we'll pick up there on Monday.

INT. MILES'S APARTMENT - EVENING   182

Miles enters his tiny apartment. He loosens his tie and
puts down his satchel.

On his way to the kitchen, he presses a button on his
ANSWERING MACHINE. As it plays, he opens the
REFRIGERATOR and looks inside.

> ANSWERING MACHINE
> *One new message.*

> MAYA'S VOICE
> Hello, Miles. It's Maya.

Miles FREEZES, not wanting to miss a single syllable.

> MAYA'S VOICE (CONT'D)
> Thanks for your letter. I would have
> called you sooner, but I think I've
> needed some time to think about
> everything that happened and what you
> wrote to me. Another reason I didn't
> call sooner is that I wanted to finish
> your book, which I finally did last
> night.

Miles's heart pounds.

                    MAYA'S VOICE (CONT'D)
          I think it's really lovely, Miles.
          You're so good with words. Who cares if
          it's not getting published? There are so
          many beautiful and painful things about
          it. Did you really go through all that?
          It must have been awfully hard. And the
          sister character -- Jesus, what a wreck.
          But I have to say I was really confused
          by the ending. Did the father finally
          commit suicide, or what? It's driving me
          crazy. And the title.

183   **INT./EXT. SAAB -- DAY**   183

THROUGH THE WINDSHIELD --

We see ourselves taking the BUELLTON EXIT.

                    MAYA'S VOICE
          Anyway, it's turned cold and rainy here
          lately. But I like winter. So listen,
          if you ever do decide to come up here
          again, you should let me know. I would
          say stop by the Hitching Post, but to
          tell you the truth I'm not sure how much
          longer I'm going to be working there.
          I'm going to graduate soon so I'll
          probably relocate. We'll see.

184   **EXT. MAYA'S APARTMENT BUILDING - DAY**   184

Miles climbs the wooden steps and approaches Maya's back
door.

                    MAYA'S VOICE
          Anyway, like I said, I really loved your
          novel. Don't give up, Miles. Keep
          writing. You're really good. Hope
          you're well. Bye.

Miles takes a breath. Finally he KNOCKS.

                         THE END

STUDY GUIDE

PREPARED BY THE SCREENWRITERS

1. Before beginning his journey, Miles finds himself forced to move his car. How often in modern life must we move our own cars, both literally and figuratively? How can we avoid this?

2. What is the basis of Jack and Miles's friendship? What does Jack represent to Miles, and vice-versa? What does Miles mean when he says, "Don't open it now. I've been saving it?"

3. In screenplay format, *Sideways* is 136 pages long. Do you think it's fair that the authors were allowed to write a script this long? If not, why? Is is fair to cheat on margins? What makes you think you could do any better?

4. At the screenplay's onset, Jack seems certain about his impending marriage, yet later he sprays his feet before asking Miles whether he (Miles) possesses other shoes. How does Jack come to question the choices he has made? Is Jack intuitive or instinctive? In your opinion, does he deserve to be called an artist?

5. What is the basis of Miles's affinity for Pinot Noir? Why does he criticize Cabernet Franc when in fact the special wine he's been saving for years—a 1961 Cheval Blanc—is made entirely of Cabernet Franc? What do you treasure in your own life that you secretly despise?

6. Much of *Sideways* is about condemning the sin but not the sinner, yet acts of reprisal are constant and stinging. Together with the themes of infidelity and atavism, what are the authors saying about the nature of revenge across generations and continents? How does this relate to harvest, fermentation and bottling?

7. Four men are adrift in a tiny boat: a doctor, a lawyer, a priest and a screenwriter. Can you make a joke out of this?

8. Discuss the character of Miles's mother. What does she represent to Miles? How do the photographs on her dresser symbolize her attachment to a bygone way of life? Why does she tell Jack, "I just remember you jogging?" Why does Miles admonish Jack not to "wake her up"?

9. Before their date with Maya and Stephanie, Jack and Miles change their clothes. Later Jack dreads calling his fiancée, Miles eats Chinese food, and near the end of their journey the two friends sit together in a Jacuzzi. By what techniques do the authors help us believe such an unlikely series of events?

10. What does Miles's sister Wendy do for a living? How does this make Miles feel? What is the overall moral tone of their relationship?

11. Ten million dollars has been buried somewhere in North America. Throughout the screenplay there are clues to its location. Can you find the money? If so, will you give it to charity or keep it?

12. In the screenplay for David Lynch's *The Elephant Man*, the protagonist confronts a mob that is chasing him with the chilling line "I am not an animal!" Is he standing up for himself or just trying to goad them into a game of twenty questions? How might Harper Lee have handled the same situation had it occurred in *To Kill A Mockingbird*?

13. When asked to give his opinion as to what type of wedding cake Jack and Christine should serve at their wedding, Miles responds, "I prefer the dark." Why doesn't he say chocolate?

14. Turn to your study-group neighbor and find something to compliment about his or her wardrobe. Now criticize the hairstyle. How do you feel? What about Miles? Jack?

15. Who the hell do you think you are and how did you get past the receptionist?

FROM BOOK TO FILM
BY REX PICKETT

In late September of 1999, Alexander Payne phoned me and said, "Rex. The King. I loved your novel *Sideways*. It's going to be my next movie." (As it turned out, *About Schmidt* was his next movie, and I would have to anxiously wait another four years.) The call came completely out of the blue. It had been almost a year since my then book-to-film agent, Jess Taylor, working at the same agency as Payne's agent, had pitched the project to him. The manuscript had also been submitted fairly widely to film production companies and the top tier of publishing houses with enthusiastic representation on both coasts. Five months later, Jess Taylor was having a difficult time in Hollywood and abruptly left the business. My literary agent at Curtis Brown had pulled the novel and persuaded me to rewrite it.

Unbeknownst to me, my orphaned manuscript had been sitting at the bottom of a pile of scripts and books at Payne's office, unread. Fortunately for me, Payne's intern, a young man named Brian Beery, finally read it and recommended it to Alexander with a ringing endorsement. On a flight back from the Edinburgh Film Festival, Alexander finally cracked it open. Evidently he liked what he read because when he disembarked from the plane he rushed to a pay phone and called his agent. All hell broke loose.

In late March of 2003, a messenger delivered the first draft of Alexander Payne and Jim Taylor's adaptation of my novel. I remember setting it on my desk and just staring at it for an hour, terrified to read it, afraid that it would be: (a) a vitiation of what I had written; (b) disappointing and that no one would want to finance it; or (c) so nakedly honest that I would disintegrate in the face of its highly personal nature. When I finally, haltingly, read it, I was astonished at how close to my novel it was. *About Schmidt* bore almost no resemblance to the novel, and *Election* took quite a few liberties with the source material as well, so I wasn't prepared for an adaptation that was so faithful.

In between the first and second drafts, Alexander, Jim, and I took a "research" trip up to the Santa Ynez Valley wine country. Alexander and I had been up together several times before, but Jim had never seen the setting for the script he was collaborating on. We meandered from tasting room to tasting room, talking about, among other topics, the script. They told me that they wrote it very quickly. But it was obvious from how tight the first draft was that they had been thinking about the material for a long time. In my writing career, I've discovered that if I let ideas germinate, allowing characters to come fully alive and inhabit my imagination, when I finally sit down to write, it usually comes out in a torrent, and it is often my most honest, and successful, work. A year later, in an e-mail, Jim confided to me that it was the easiest adaptation they'd ever done "because the material was just there in the novel. All we had to do was choose and lift."

Over dinner, at the end of a lovely day, they asked me what I thought about the first draft and I said to them: "I think you had to make a film about maturity…"—i.e., *About Schmidt*—"first in order to be able to find a way to make a film about immaturity." They both laughed acknowledgment, but I truly believe, after having now seen a nearly final cut of the resultant film, that the two of them have deepened as writers and have, as a result, brought a greater gravitas to *Sideways* than I was expecting.

Watching the film in a screening room at 20th Century Fox, I saw scene after scene from my book unfold onto the screen largely intact. Oh, sure, they were abridged and altered, owing to the exigencies of film and the necessity of time compression that the medium mandates, but it was startlingly true to my book. Most novelists whose books are turned into movies are lucky to see even a fraction of their original ideas and characters committed to celluloid; many find their novels unrecognizable in the screen version, smile ruefully at their big paycheck, and complain silently to their friends. So, to have a filmmaker of Alexander Payne's caliber honor my novel with such a faithful cinematic representation was nothing short of self-satisfying.

Just how faithful is Alexander and Jim's adaptation? *Sideways* is a novel about two longtime friends who are heading to a wedding. One of them, Jack, is to be married and the other, Miles (the first-person narrator), is his best man. The novel employs a chapter structure that begins with each day of the week that they spend before the wedding. Alexander and Jim elected to maintain this chapter structure in the movie, superimposing the days of the week over the opening scene of each new day. I couldn't believe it when I read it in the script, and continued to be surprised when I saw it on the screen (where it could have easily been scrapped). Watching the movie, I felt like I was peeking into my book but instead of seeing words I was witnessing a veritable visualization of the words themselves.

In addition, because the book is written in the first person, I did not have the luxury to take the reader outside the bounds of the narrator. But, in the script, Alexander and Jim were afforded that luxury and could have gone off, sans narrator, with any of the other characters, particularly Jack. But they chose to stay entirely with Miles (played by Paul Giamatti). I thought this was an odd, but brave choice, and wasn't even sure that they were conscious of it. When I pointed it out to Alexander, he explained simply, "It's Miles's story." By opting to remain, essentially, in the first person, he imparts to the film an introspective tone that it might not have otherwise had in another director's hands. It's this introspective tone—which is a hallmark of my book—that balances beautifully against the bawdy, comic side of the movie—a balance that I originally feared the movie might not have. Like a well-made wine, *Sideways* has a deft balance of bracing acidity and salacious fruit. If it was just bracing acidity we would quickly weary of it; if it was just salacious fruit, we would soon grow sated by its absence of depth and complexity.

There *are* changes in the movie, of course. Miles in the novel comes across more as a free spirit, a novelist manqué, chronically unemployed, living precariously on the edge. In the script, by giving Miles a "real" occupation and making him a middle-school teacher, he becomes less the bohemian living by his wits and more of a man mired in a middle-class existence, pedaling in neutral, living from paycheck to paycheck, hoping against hope that his magnum opus of a novel, *The Day After Yesterday*, will be picked up by a publisher and he'll be spared the drudgery of grading eighth-grade papers until retirement. Miles in the novel is more of a dreamer, a fringe character, someone who once had a brush with fame in Hollywood as a screenwriter, while Miles in the script has never had anything really exciting happen to him in his life. As a result, he comes across more as an average Joe, a character that Payne and Taylor are more fond of—and apparently, judging by their earlier work, more interested in exploring cinematically.

There's another significant change—or evolution in Alexander's sensibility—that bears noting. His first three films were all shot in Nebraska (with a few minor forays to Colorado and New York) and usually, it seems, around wintertime. As a result, they all have a similarly, but consciously, intended palette of muted colors. The mostly monochromatic look of these films is underscored by Payne's penchant for drab locations: depersonalized budget motels, fluorescent-lit offices, kitschy fast-food emporiums, desolate streets and even more desolate residences. In contrast, however, *Sideways* was shot in the gorgeous, Tuscany-resembling, Santa Ynez Valley in its most beautiful season, fall, when the vineyards are leafed out and drooping with fully ripened grape clusters. As a result, his fourth feature showcases a lush, romantic look. Indeed, *Sideways* is Alexander's first film to deal with romance in a non-satirical way—incipient attraction, awkward first kisses, marriage jitters, the pain of divorce, and starting anew. Of course, it's what the novel is about, but I found it interesting that he would choose to make such an opulent-looking film (he even changed directors of photography) and not be afraid of his—he'll cringe when he reads this—sentimental and feminine side.

When he was cast, Paul Giamatti was not the Miles I had originally imagined. I had envisioned a somewhat roguish enfant terrible (Sean Penn comes to mind) playing the last notes on his out-of-tune sax. But when I saw the film, I realized that Alexander had seen the character a few shades differently—as I said, more the common man—and that Paul, with his hangdog physiognomy and unprepossessing look, perfectly embodied that tonal difference. Thomas Haden Church as the lovable, but wayward, Jack was everything I imagined that character to be and he did not disappoint. He perfectly portrays the character I wrote as larger than life, effusively demonstrative, not the brightest bulb in the grid, but not devoid of intuitive feeling either. Virginia Madsen was honestly more than I imagined for the female lead, Maya. She infuses her character with all the verisimilitude of an angel, and she has several memorable screen moments, particularly a lyrical speech on wine (that is all Alexander and Jim!) that is both romantic and erotically charged at the same time. In a lesser role, Sandra Oh is perfect as the promiscuous coquette, Stephanie. But when I saw the film, it was Giamatti's performance that surprised me. His bitterness toward his lot in life—again, a tonal shade different from the novel Miles who is more self-deprecatingly resigned—which I feared would make him unsympathetic, turns to a heartbreaking empathy and, finally, a profound sadness welling up out of him—and us. This sentiment is clearly in the novel, but it's a credit to Paul for finding it emotionally in his acting, and a credit to Alexander and Jim for scavenging for it wherever they could find it in the novel and underscoring it on the screen.

Alexander Payne is a highly educated and articulate artist. He's bored easily with confabulation and will often abruptly shift the topic of conversation to films (he is a cinephile par excellence and sees practically everything), to literature, politics, or in-depth discussions of wine-making, or whatever his far-ranging mind seizes on. He is ardently peripatetic, appears interested in everything, and hungers for experience. He brandishes a laser wit, but it's tempered by his genuine, selfless interest in others. I think he saw in Miles, the eighth-grade school teacher/novelist wannabe (that he and Jim transformed him into), the portent of an unfulfilled life that artists who don't make it will be subjected to, and of which I suspect he was once terrified. He empathizes with this character precisely because he knows all too intimately how many talented people, whose dreams to be filmmakers or writers don't pan out, end up in dead-end existences, toiling away for nothing, their aspirations and spirits quashed. Though Payne can be wickedly satirical, sometimes pitilessly so, he ultimately feels for the plight of the common man. And it is these sad sack souls, beaten down by, and adrift and dispirited in, life, who inspire him.

I have often heard that seeing the movie is almost never as satisfying as reading the book. After going through countless rewrites and mind-numbing copy-edits of the novel and poring over four drafts of Alexander and Jim's adaptation, I will confess to a dearth of perspective. However, after seeing their final creation, I unequivocally believe that Alexander has crafted a film that honors, if I may be so bold, the depth and complexity in characters I was going for when I wrote *Sideways*, which was published in June 2004. It's as if he went in with a scalpel and excised everything but the heart, while staying true to the tenor of the book. As a skilled filmmaker and screenwriter he obviously knew what he was looking for and had a vision he was operating under. Like the novel, there is comedy galore, but the film is, in my opinion, more serious and, as a result, possibly more profound than the book as a whole, a true alchemy of the latter's strongest elements.

As of this writing, the film is still three months from release. I don't know what the critical reception will be, but I can ingenuously report there is no more fortunate novelist (whose book was turned into a film) than me. I had one of the finest filmmakers of his generation, given free rein by the auteur-run Fox Searchlight headed by the courageous Peter Rice, faithfully adapt my novel with all the respect (and more!) that it deserved. The sun often only breaks through the clouds once in a writer's life and I stand, however ephemerally, basking in its rays.

July 2004

CAST AND CREW CREDITS

FOX SEARCHLIGHT PICTURES Presents
A MICHAEL LONDON Production

SIDEWAYS

PAUL GIAMATTI   THOMAS HADEN CHURCH

VIRGINIA MADSEN   SANDRA OH

Directed by ALEXANDER PAYNE	Produced by MICHAEL LONDON	Film Editor KEVIN TENT, A.C.E.
Screenplay by ALEXANDER PAYNE & JIM TAYLOR	Co–Producer GEORGE PARRA Director of Photography	Costume Designer WENDY CHUCK Music Supervisor
Based on the Novel by REX PICKETT	PHEDON PAPAMICHAEL, ASC Production Designer JANE ANN STEWART	DONDI BASTONE Music by ROLFE KENT

CAST

Miles . . . . PAUL GIAMATTI
Jack. . . . . THOMAS HADEN CHURCH
Maya . . . . VIRGINIA MADSEN
Stephanie . . . . SANDRA OH
Miles's Mother . . . . MARYLOUISE BURKE
Victoria . . . . JESSICA HECHT
Cammi . . . . MISSY DOTY
Cammi's Husband . . . . MC GAINEY
Christine Erganian . . . . ALYSIA REINER
Mrs. Erganian . . . . SHAKÉ TOUKHMANIAN
Mike Erganian . . . . DUKE MOOSEKIAN
Miles's Building Manager . . . . . ROBERT COVARRUBIAS
Gary the Bartender . . . . PATRICK GALLAGHER
Stephanie's Mother . . . . STEPHANIE FARACY
Frass Canyon Pourer . . . . JOE MARINELLI
Chris at Sanford . . . . CHRIS BURROUGHS
Evelyn Berman-Silverman . . . . TONI HOWARD
Armenian Priest . . . REV. FR. KHOREN BABOUCHIAN
Ken Cortland . . . . LEE BROOKS
Leslie Brough . . . . PETER DENNIS
Foxen Winery Pourer . . . . ALISON HERSON
Vacationing Dr. Walt Hendricks . . . . PHIL REEVES
Obnoxious Golfer . . . . ROB TROW
Los Olivos Waitress . . . . LACEY RAE
Barista . . . . CESAR "CHEESER" RAMOS
Reciting Eighth Grader . . . . DANIEL ROGERS
Siena . . . . NATALIE CARTER
Mini-Mart Owner . . . . SIMON KASSIS
Armenian Deacon . . . . SEVAG KENDIRJIAN

Acoustic Guitarist . . . . JAREN COLER
Stunt Coordinator . . . . TOM ELLIOTT
Stunts by . . . . . STEVE HOLLADAY, GARY K. PRICE,
MARK STEFANICH

CREW

Unit Production Manager . . . . GINGER SLEDGE
First Assistant Director . . . . GEORGE PARRA
Second Assistant Director . . . . NICK SATRIANO
Music Supervisor . . . . DONDI BASTONE
Sound Design and Supervision . . . . . . FRANK GAETA
Re-Recording Mixers . . . . PATRICK CYCCONE
TONY LAMBERTI
Music Editor . . . . RICHARD FORD
2nd Unit Director of Photography . . . . . JENNIFER LANE
Factotum . . . . TRACY BOYD
Post Production Supervisor . . . . STEVE BARNETT
Art Director . . . . . . TIMOTHY "TK" KIRKPATRICK
Set Decorators . BARBARA HABERECHT, LISA FISCHER
Assistant Art Director . . . . MASAKO MASUDA
Camera Operator . . . . PAUL G. SANCHEZ
First Assistant Camera . . . . BOB HALL
Second Assistant Camera . . . . PHIL SHANAHAN
Loader . . . . DANIEL McFADDEN
Sound Mixer . . . . JOSE ANTONIO GARCIA
Boom Operator . . . . JONATHAN FUH
Utility Sound . . . . STEVEN KLINGHOFFER
Script Supervisor . . . . REBECCA ROBERTSON-SZWAJA
Chief Lighting Technician . . . . . . RAFAEL SANCHEZ
Best Boy Electric . . . . JAREK GORCZYCKI
Key Grip . . . . RAY GARCIA

Best Boy Grip . . . . DONIS RHODEN
Dolly Grip . . . . ANTONIO GARRIDO
Costume Supervisor . . . . LORI STILSON
Costumer. . . . . JEANNINE BOURDAGHS
Set Costumers . . . . . . SUSAN STRUBEL, ERIN LENK
Property Master . . . . JEFFREY M. O'BRIEN
Assistant Property Master. . . . . . . DERRICK HINMAN
2nd Assistant Property Master . . . . . DENISE M. CIARCIA
Dept. Head Makeup Artist . . . . . . JEANNE VAN PHUE
Assistant Makeup Artist . . . . PAMELA PHILLIPS
Key Hair Stylist. . . . . BRIDGET M. COOK
Assistant Hair Stylist. . . . . NICOLE FRANK
Set Decoration Leadman . . . . MARK WOODS
On Set Dresser . . . . CYNTHIA REBMAN
Set Decoration Buyer . . . . KRISTEN McCARRON
Armenian Liaison and Coordinator . . . MARAL DJEREJIAN
Transportation Coordinator . . . . GARY EDELMAN
Transportation Captain . . . . CHARLIE RAMIREZ
Location Managers . . JEREMY ALTER, JOHN LATENSER V
Special Effects Coordinator . . . . TERRY FRAZEE
Construction Coordinator . . . . MIKE DIERSING
Assistant Production Coordinators . . . . ERIN FERGUSON
KRIS OLSON
Art Department Coordinator . . . . . KATHLEEN WALKER
Clearance Coordinator. . . . . BONNIE BARABAS
Marine Coordinator . . . . C. RANSOM WALROD
Production Supervisor . . . . YVONNE YACONELLI
Production Accountant . . . . . . MARSHA L. SWINTON
1st Assistant Accountant . . . . SHERRI GOLDMAN
2nd Assistant Accountant . . . . . JENNIFER VAN HOVEN
Payroll Accountant . . . . TRISH VENGOECHEA
Post Accountants . . . . . . KIM BODNER, CHRIS STARK
Assistants to Mr. Payne . . . . EVAN ENDICOTT
RACHEL ANNE FLEISCHER
Assistant to Mr. London . . . . KHRISTINA KRAVAS
Assistant to Mr. Parra . . REBECCA WHITESELL LaFOND
Wine Consultant . . . . BRAD IWANAGA
Lamp Operators . . LEE AUERBACH, ALEX J. CASTILLO,
STEVE COLGROVE, JEFFREY M. HALL,
PATRICK R. HOESCHEN
Company Grips . . . . DAVID ARINIELLO,
T. DANIEL SCARINGI, DOUGLAS L. WALL,
MARK WOJCIECHOWSKI
On Set Medic . . . . KERI LITTLEDEER
2nd 2nd Assistant Director . . . . SUSAN WALTER
Set Production Assistants . . . . NICK FITZGERALD, PHIL
DeSANTI, JULIE A. ELDER, CANDELA FIGUEIRA,
BRIAN BEERY
Office Production Assistants . . . . . BRIAN A. HOFFMAN,
JENNIFER MOSLEY, YASEMIN KASIM
Art Department Production Assistants. . . . . . GERASIMOS
CHRISTOFORATOS, GABRIEL MANN, JON REYNOLDS

Property Production Assistant . . . . JENNIFER HAMILTON
Craft Service . . . . METI KUSARI
Unit Still Photographer . . MERIE WEISMILLER WALLACE
Unit Publicists . . . .
EDDIE MICHAELS & ASSOCIATES/ ERIK BRIGHT
Caterer . . . . TONY'S FOOD SERVICE
Casting Assistant . . . . JESSIE SALKA
Extras Casting - LA SMITH & WEBSTER-DAVIS CASTING
Set Dressers . . LEAH FERRARINI, MARK "TRAVIS" LITTLE,
JOANIE MEYER, TRISTAN OLIVER, NILS THYRRING
Set Decoration Production Assistant . . COCO HARRISON
Assistant Location Managers . . KYLE "SNAPPY" OLIVER,
ANTON PARDOE, ALBIE SALSICH
Key Location Assistant . . . . KENDRA LIEDLE
Location Assistant . . . . JOSH MANN
Additional Set Production Assistants . . DANIELA De CARLO
SIMON FERRER
Accounting Clerk . . . . ARRON PAWLOWICZ
Production Office Intern . . . . PAUL CAVANAUGH
Intern to Mr. London . . . . ANNE ELISE SCHMIDT
Location Interns . . . . MIKE HOOD, KAHLAH MACEDO
JESSICA SZEJN
First Assistant Editor . . . . ALEXIS SEYMOUR
Assistant Editor . . . . LAURA RINDNER
Apprentice Editor. . . . . DAVID BERMAN
Post Production Assistant . . BENJAMIN "JAMI" PHILBRICK
Editorial Cat . . . . LULU
ADR/Dialogue Supervisor . . . . DAVID BACH
Dialogue Editors . . RUSSELL FARMARCO, ROB GETTY,
PATRICK GIRAUDI
Sound Effects Editors . . DEREK VANDERHORST, JAMES
ALDRIGE, CARLOS GUTIERREZ
Foley Editor. . . . . JOHN STEWART
Foley Artists . . CATHERINE HARPER, CHRIS ORYAMA
Assistant Sound Editors . . . . . . DENNIS TWITTY, PAUL
HACKNER, LUIS GALDAMES
ADR Mixers . . . RON BEDROSIAN, WELDON BROWN,
COLIN McCLELLAN, SHAYNA BROWN
ADR Recordists . JULIO CARMONA , DARYL LATHROP,
EDGAR CAISSIE
Foley Mixer. . . . . RANDY SINGER
Recordists . CHRISTOPHER SIDOR, MATT COLLERAN
Stage Engineers . . . . BILL RITTER, JIM ALBERT
Post Production Sound by . . . . SOUND FOR FILM
Rerecorded at . . . . TODD-AO - HOLLYWOOD
Score Recorded in Hollywood, California at . . . .
O'HENRY STUDIOS, CONWAY STUDIOS
Score Mixed at . . . . SIGNET SOUND
ADR Stages. . . TODD-AO - HOLLYWOOD & RADFORD
DELUXE SOUND - TORONTO
TEQUILA MOCKINGBIRD - AUSTIN
Foley Stage . . . . PARAMOUNT STUDIOS

Orchestration & Score Coordination . . . TONY BLONDAL
Programming . . . STEPHEN COLEMAN, NICK SOUTH
Conductor . . . . STEPHEN COLEMAN
Musicians' Contractor . . . . DAN SAVANT
Music Copying . . . . ERIC STONEROOK
Scoring Mixer . . . . GREG TOWNLEY
Mix Assistant . . . . TOM HARDISTY
Recording Assistants . . . . . . CHRISTINE SIROIS, SETH
WALDMANN, KEVIN SZYMANSKI
Assistant Music Editors . . . JASON RUDER, OLIVER HUG
THE SIDEWAYS JAZZ ORCHESTRA
Piano . . . . RON FEUER
Vibes . . . . ROGER BURN
Saxes . . . . DAN HIGGINS
Trumpet . . . . DAN SAVANT
Flutes . . . . PEDRO EUSTACHE
Drums . . . . WILL KENNEDY
Bass . . . . PAUL MORIN
Percussion . . . . ALEX ACUÑA
Percussion . . . . LUIS CONTE
Percussion . . . . RICARDO "TIKI" PASILLAS
Melodica, Guitar . . . . ROLFE KENT
ADDITIONAL MUSICIANS
Saxes . . . . BRIAN SCANLON
Flutes . . . . JUSTO ALMARIO
Piano . . . . TOM RANIER
Bass . . . . KENNY WILD
Bass . . . . DAVE CARPENTER
Drums . . . . NICK VINCENT
Percussion . . . . DANNY GRECO
Saxes/Flutes . . . . GARY FOSTER
Trumpet . . . . BOB SUMMERS
Wedding Vocalist . . . . HEGHINE (HELEN) HARBOYAN
Wedding Organist . . . . GOHAR TORANYAN
Color Timer . . . . MATO
Negative Cutter . . . . GARY BURRITT
Preview Engineer . . . . LEE TUCKER
Main Title Design by . . . RIGHT LOBE DESIGN GROUP
Digital Opticals & End Titles by . . CUSTOM FILM EFFECTS
Digital Visual Effects . . . . FLASH FILM WORKS
Additional Camera Operator . . . . MAURICE K. McGUIRE
Additional 1st Assistant Camera . . . . . PAUL THERIAULT
Additional 2nd Assistant Camera . . . . . . DAN SQUIRES
JACQUELINE J. NIVENS
Additional Camera Loader . . . . . . ALEXANDRA LUCKA
Camera Intern . . . . TARI SEGAL
24 Frame Playback Operator . . . . PAUL MURPHEY
Rigging Gaffer . . . . RODGER MEILINK
Best Boy Rigging Electric . . . . SEAN M. HIGGINS
Rigging Electric . . . . KEVIN BARRERA
Rigging Key Grip . . . . BLAKE PIKE
Best Boy Rigging Grip . . . . TONY SOMMO
Rigging Grip . . . . JACK KORBEL

General Construction Foreman . . . . . BRENT T. REGAN
Foremen . . . . . RICHARD ECKOLS, SCOTT E. HANDT
Propmakers . . . . . JEFF SHEWBERT, KEVIN DIERSING
Toolman . . . . VLAD PELINOVSCHI
Labor Foreman . . . . WILLIE HASPEL
Lead Paint Foreman . . . . ANNE HYVARINEN
Painters . . . . . . MARCO GILSON, KAREN GREENE
Standby Painter . . . . ANTHONY GAUDIO
Signwriter . . . . MICHAEL P. WALSH
Construction Medics . . . . DONNA LEE KILLINS
MICHAEL HIRD
Greens Foreman . . . . JEFF BROWN
Greens Coordinator . . . . FRANK McELDOWNEY
Special Effects Assistant Coordinator . DONALD L. FRAZEE
Special Effects Technician . . . . KAI SHELTON
Insert Car Driver . . . . BILL ISAACSON
Studio Teachers . . . . . . JIM HARTZ, LINDA STANLEY
Projectionist . . . . TOM AJAR
Cook Assistants   MIGUEL PEREZ, DAVID WESTENBERG
Voice Casting . . . . THE REEL TEAM
Voice Actors . . W.K. STRATTON, WENDY HOFFMANN,
RICHARD JANNONE, KATE CARLIN, SALLY BROOKS,
ANYA MARINA, RACHEL CRANE, NICHOLAS GUEST,
AL RODRIGO, PAUL PAPE
Camera Cranes and Dollies by . . . .
CHAPMAN/LEONARD STUDIO EQUIPMENT, INC.
Camera Dollies provided by . . . . J.L. FISHER, INC.
Super Technocrane provided by . . . .
PANAVISION REMOTE SYSTEMS
Camera Car . . . . THE SHOTMAKER COMPANY

THURSDAY NIGHT AT PASQUALE'S
Written and Performed by Astrid Cowan
Courtesy of Astron Records

ONE YEAR AFTER
Written and Performed by Uli Lenz
Courtesy of Arkadia Entertainment Corp.
By arrangement with Position Music

UMBRELLA INDOORS
Written and Performed by Uli Lenz
Courtesy of Arkadia Entertainment Corp.
By arrangement with Position Music

FACE TO FACE
Written by Stephen Lang, Jamie Dunlap and Scott Nickoley
Performed by Molly Pasutti
Courtesy of Marc Ferrari/MasterSource

FEARLESS LOVE
Written by Dillon O'Brian
Performed by Bonnie Raitt
Courtesy of Capitol Records
Under license from EMI Film & Television Music

146

SLEEPING PILL
Written by Dean Wareham, Sean Eden, Justin Harwood and
Stanley Demeski
Performed by Luna
Courtesy of Elektra Entertainment Group
By arrangement with Warner Strategic Marketing

SYMBIOSIS
Written by Claus Ogermann
Performed by Bill Evans
Courtesy of Verve Records
Under license from Universal Music Enterprises

TWO TICKETS TO PARADISE
Written and Performed by Eddie Money
Courtesy of Omnibus Records & Tapes,
A division of Music Sales Corp
o/b/o Eddie Money

NEW HAVEN COMET
Written by Dean Wareham, Sean Eden,
Lee Wall and Britta Phillips
Performed by Luna
Courtesy of Jetset Records
By arrangement with Ocean Park Music Group

FADED AWAY
Written by Jamie Dunlap, Lisa Furr and Scott Nickoley
Performed by Lisa Furr
Courtesy of Marc Ferrari/Mastersource

RECUERDOS de la ALHAMBRA
Written by Francisco Tarrega
Arranged and Performed by Jaren Coler

THE HONKY TONK WINE
Written and Performed by Carl Sonny Leyland
Courtesy of High Tone Records
By arrangement with Ocean Park Music Group

SAD SONGS
Words and Music by David Allen Klingenberger
and Edward M. Rudolph
Performed by Deke Dickerson
Courtesy of Songs of D.K.

SNORTIN' WHISKEY
Written by Pat Thrall and Pat Travers
Performed by Pat Travers
Courtesy of Universal Records
Under license from Universal Music Enterprises

NAYYA EE MEZ
Traditional
Performed by Gomidas Vartabed Komitas

SOUNDTRACK ON NEW LINE RECORDS

The producers wish to thank the following for their assistance:
HOLY CROSS ARMENIAN APOSTOLIC CHURCH
REEM ACRA BRIDAL

KIRK IRWIN PHOTOGRAPHY
JUDITH HALE GALLERY
THE CITY OF LOS OLIVOS
SANTA BARBARA CONFERENCE & VISITORS
BUREAU & FILM COMMISSION
SOLVANG DANISH VILLAGE CONFERENCE
& VISITORS BUREAU
THE CITY OF BUELLTON
SANTA BARBARA COUNTY
THE SANTA BARBARA VINTNERS ASSOCIATION
THE SANFORD, KALYRA, FOXEN, FIRESTONE,
ANDREW MURRAY and FESS PARKER WINERIES

No California oak trees were harmed
in the making of this motion picture.

Footage from "GRAPES OF WRATH" courtesy of Twentieth
Century Fox. All rights reserved.

HELL'S BATTLEFIELD: THE BATTLE OF THE BULGE
courtesy of The History Channel

CODENAME: KIDS NEXT DOOR and all related characters
and elements are trademarks of Cartoon Network © 2003.
A Time Warner Company. All Rights Reserved.

MTV's "The Grind" used with permission by MTV. ©1996
MTV Networks. All Rights Reserved.

Golf footage courtesy of THE GOLF CHANNEL

Marketplace® Copyright 2004 American Public Media. All
rights reserved. Used by permission of American Public Media.

Excerpts from "A Separate Peace" used by Permission of Curtis
Brown, Ltd. Copyright © 1959 by John Knowles.
All rights reserved.

Filmed with PANAVISION ® Cameras & Lenses

Color & Processing by FOTOKEM

Prints by DELUXE®

RELEASED BY TWENTIETH CENTURY FOX

BIOGRAPHIES

Alexander Payne was born in Rome to a sculptor father and historian mother and was raised largely in Menorca. He left Harvard after two years to work as a longshoreman, a waiter, a bus driver, a pool man, and a translator. *Sideways* is his fourth feature film as co-writer and director. He is currently at work on his second volume of poetry. His first, *Shadings and Shadowings,* was published in 1991.

Jim Taylor was born in Seattle. His father was a dentist. If anyone has seen the glove he lost at the Göthenberg film festival in 1996, please contact the publisher.

Rex Pickett is a screenwriter and published his first novel *Sideways* in June 2004 with St. Martin's Press.

Peter Travers is the film critic for *Rolling Stone* magazine.

Alexander Payne & Jim Taylor Filmography:

Citizen Ruth (1996)

Election (1999)

About Schmidt (2002)

Sideways (2004)